D1443372

For more than forty years,
Yearling has been the leading name
in classic and award-winning literature
for young readers.

Yearling books feature children's
favorite authors and characters,
providing dynamic stories of adventure,
humor, history, mystery, and fantasy.

Trust Yearling paperbacks to entertain,
inspire, and promote the love of reading
in all children.

# PHYLLIS REYNOLDS NAYLOR

■ ■ ■ ■ ■ ■ ■ ■

# THE GIRLS' REVENGE

■

A YEARLING BOOK

*For Kathleen's grandchildren,*
*born to West Virginia daddies:*
*two families of girls: Katie, Elizabeth, and Caroline;*
*Kalyn;*
*one family of boys: Adam, Gavin, and Philip;*
*and one family of both: Juliann and Joseph;*
*with best wishes for happy reading,*
*especially to their grandma,*
*who always gives them books*

Published by Yearling, an imprint of Random House Children's Books
a division of Random House, Inc., New York

Yearling and the jumping horse design are registered trademarks of Random House, Inc.

Visit us on the Web! www.randomhouse.com/kids

Educators and librarians, for a variety of teaching tools, visit us at
www.randomhouse.com/teachers

ISBN: 0-440-41383-4

Reprinted by arrangement with Delacorte Press

Printed in the United States of America

October 1999

19 18 17 16 15 14

# Contents

■ ■ ■ ■ ■ ■

■ ■ ■ ■ ■ ■ ■ ■ ■ ■ ■

# One

■

# A Change in the Wind

Caroline Malloy had just hung a Christmas wreath on the door when she had a wonderful, awful thought. It was the kind of thought that made her lips curl up at the corners.

Ever since her father had moved the family to Buckman, where he was coaching the college football team for a year, Caroline had been having these thoughts. So had her two sisters, Beth, who was ten, and Eddie, who was eleven, and whose real name was Edith Ann.

Caroline herself was only eight, but she was considered precocious for her age and had skipped a grade, so she was in the same class as Wally Hatford, who lived across the river. And the wonderful, awful thought had something to do with Wally and his brothers.

She dashed back into the house, her dark ponytail flopping behind her, brown eyes snapping, and clattered upstairs to where Beth, her feet propped on the radiator and her instruction book against her knees, was attempting to knit a lavender scarf for Mother for Christmas.

"I've got a terrific idea!" Caroline said breathlessly. "Want to hear it?"

"Hmmm," said Beth, studying the page, then the wool in front of her.

*Thunk . . . thunk . . . thunk,* came a noise from the next bedroom, where Eddie was bouncing a rubber ball on the floor. Caroline decided to tell both sisters together.

"Eddie?" she called. "Want to hear my idea?"

The *thunk, thunk, thunk* grew louder as Eddie ambled in from the next room, bouncing the ball with one hand and holding her Christmas gift list in the other. She was the tallest of the Malloy girls, with long legs, short blond hair, and brown eyes that matched Caroline's. "Well?" she said, waiting, her attention still on the list.

"My idea," began Caroline, who loved an audience more than she loved chocolate cream pie, "is to give each of the Hatford brothers a Christmas present. From us to them. Beautifully wrapped, of course . . ."

"Are you nuts?" asked Beth, her feet thudding to the floor in shock.

"But *inside* each box will be something really awful."

"Like what?" asked Eddie, finally looking up.

Caroline hadn't figured that part out yet. She was thinking about the time, just after the Malloys had moved to West Virginia, when the Hatford boys had dumped dead birds and stuff on the girls' side of the river to make them think the water was polluted. And the time they had lured Caroline into the cellar at Oldakers' Bookstore, then stood on the trapdoor so she couldn't get out. And all the other times they had tried to make the Malloys so miserable that the girls would persuade their father to move back to Ohio when the year was up.

"I don't know," Caroline said at last. "A dead squirrel, maybe. A rotten banana. Whatever we can find to gross them out. Can't you just *see* their faces on Christmas morning, untying a bow and finding this *thing* in the box?"

She had expected her sisters to jump at the chance. She had thought Eddie, in particular, would come up with an idea even more gross than she could imagine.

Instead Eddie said, "Oh, I don't know, Caroline. These pranks are getting a little stale, aren't they?"

Caroline stuck her fingers in both ears and pulled them out quickly to unplug them. She couldn't have heard right. This was *Eddie* talking?

"Yeah, it's Christmas, after all!" said Beth. "Where's your Christmas spirit?"

Caroline blinked, then blinked again. This couldn't be happening! Since her family had moved to Buckman and the Hatford boys had tried to drive them out, she had never had so much fun and excitement. She'd thought that Beth and Eddie felt the same way.

"What's *happened* to you two?" she cried. "I thought we'd been having fun! I thought we were going to drive the Hatfords so bonkers they'd wish

3

they'd never messed with us! Don't you remember all the fun we had pretending I'd died and you just dumped my body in the river? And the time we climbed on their roof and howled and . . ."

"Softball season will be coming up in a couple of months, and I've got other things on my mind," said Eddie. "I *really* want to get on the team. If I get a bunch of guys mad at me, it's not going to help."

In desperation, Caroline turned to Beth, but Beth said, "I don't see how we can be mean to them after they invited us over for Thanksgiving dinner."

"Easy!" Caroline bleated. "Easy, easy, easy! Right this minute they're probably thinking up something awful to do to us!"

"Then we'll deal with it when it happens," said Beth. "Now go away. I want to work on this scarf, and I'm making all kinds of mistakes."

Caroline was speechless. She didn't even make it as far as her room. She just sank down at the top of the stairs and blankly stared at the wall.

They were supposed to be a team! Caroline had always dreamed of having a production company when they were grown—Beth would write the script, Eddie would be the stuntwoman, and Caroline, of course, would be the star. Now she didn't know what to expect.

Nine more months before they went back to Ohio, *if* they went back at all. Only nine months to get even again and again with the Hatford boys. And don't think the boys weren't having as much fun as they were.

Well, she told herself, if Beth and Eddie weren't interested in playing one of the best tricks she'd ever thought of on the Hatfords, was there any reason she couldn't do it herself? To *one* of the Hatfords, anyway. Wally sat right in front of her in Miss Applebaum's fourth-grade class. She had to look at his stupid neck and his stupid ears six hours a day for the next six months. Wasn't she entitled to just one little joke to get even for all the stuff he had done to her? And if he hadn't done all that much, Caroline figured he'd *thought* of doing it, which was just as bad, wasn't it?

She would simply put her mind to thinking up the most hideous, horrible thing she could put in a box for Wally Hatford, and she would wrap it up in gorgeous paper and give it to him whenever she got the chance. Of course, she would have to be nice to him between now and Christmas vacation, or he'd suspect it was a joke and throw it out without looking.

And so, when Caroline went to school the next day, she said, "Hi, Wally. I like your sweater."

Actually, she didn't. It was an ugly sweater. It had reindeer on it with green antlers. She had never seen a green-antlered reindeer, and what's more, the sweater was too big for Wally. It looked as though it had once belonged to Josh or Jake, the eleven-year-old twins.

Wally looked surprised.

"Thanks," he said. "It used to be Jake's."

So far so good, thought Caroline. Every day she would pay at least one compliment to Wally Hatford so that, by the time Christmas vacation got here, he'd just have to accept her present. It would seem rude not to. And maybe, when Beth and Eddie saw how much fun they were missing, they'd go back to making life miserable for Jake and Josh as well.

The only Hatford Caroline really liked was seven-year-old Peter. He couldn't help that he was a Hatford. And he *was* sort of sweet.

After school that afternoon, when Beth and Eddie went to the library to do their homework, Caroline walked around the yard there on Island Avenue, where the Malloys were renting a house from the Benson family for a year. The Bensons had gone to Georgia temporarily, where Mr. Benson was coaching a football team and teaching college. Sort of an exchange program. It was because the Hatford boys had been best friends with the Benson boys that Wally and Jake and Josh and even Peter resented the girls' moving in.

Caroline was walking around the yard looking for ideas for a gross-out present for Wally. A stray cat that belonged more or less to the neighborhood was sitting on the driveway licking its paws. It had probably just eaten something yucky, Caroline thought. A mouse or something. A mouse with whiskers, its tail sticking out one side of the cat's mouth.

"How are you, Patches?" Caroline asked, bending down to pet the animal behind the ears. "Give me an idea for a present for Wally. Something really, really sick."

Patches only purred and licked her paws again. She had probably been mousing in the old garage. Caroline walked through the garage looking for grossness. Spiders? Worms? Garbage? Maggots? Garbage *and* maggots?

Whatever, it had to be so disgusting that Wally and his brothers would trip all over themselves trying to get even. All it would take was one really awful trick against the Malloy sisters, and the feud would be on again. She could count on it, Christmas or not.

■ ■ ■ ■ ■ ■ ■ ■ ■ ■ ■ ■

# Two

■

# December Project

Life for Wally Hatford, age nine, was going surprisingly well.

He had never expected this to happen. Ever since their best friends, the Bensons, moved to Georgia for a year, and the Whomper, the Weirdo, and the Crazie moved in, he had thought life would never be the same again.

Eddie Malloy, the Whomper, could hit a ball from one side of Buckman to the other, practically; Beth, the Weirdo, read the kind of books that were meant to be read at night in a graveyard; and Caroline—well, having Caroline Malloy sitting right behind you in school, breathing on the back of your neck, meant that anything at all could happen.

Wally, unlike his twin brothers, Josh and Jake, did not seem to need a lot of excitement to make him happy. He was happy just to have one day go the same as the one before, peaceful, unhurried, with plenty of time to dream and imagine, to think about what he did the past summer and plan how he would spend his next vacation.

"He'll never set the world on fire, but he's steady," Wally overheard his mom say to his aunt once. And that was just fine with him.

But when the Malloys moved in, he forgot what peaceful was. He forgot what quiet was. When a strange animal, possibly a cougar, was sighted around Buckman—an animal the newspaper nicknamed an abaguchie—Wally even dreamed that the animal had carried off Caroline, and he would never have to feel her poking him in the back again with her pencil.

But suddenly, as though she had changed overnight from a dragon to a duchess, Caroline Malloy turned polite. She turned kind. In fact, she turned downright strange.

"Nice pen, Wally," she said on this particular day as Wally was trying out a pen with five colors of ink in it, which he had bought at the five-and-dime.

"Thanks," said Wally.

"It was really cold this morning, wasn't it?" Caroline went on. "Do you usually have snow here at Christmas?"

"Sometimes, but not always," Wally told her.

"Back in Ohio we usually did. I guess we'll have to wait and see."

Miss Applebaum was taking the roll now, so Wally didn't answer. But he was thinking about what Caroline had just said. Did that mean that she and her sisters were getting to like it here? Did that mean they were going to *stay*? Could he stand it if his best friends in the whole world decided to spend the rest of their lives in Georgia?

Now Miss Applebaum was talking about something she called the December project. She made it sound as though the December project were the biggest thing since the space shuttle. She made it sound as though, if you flunked the December project, you could say goodbye to fifth grade. Everybody had to do it, and you had to choose partners and work together as a team.

Caroline's hand shot up in the air, and Miss Applebaum looked at her curiously.

"Yes, Caroline?"

"I choose Wally Hatford," she said.

Wally felt all the blood in his body rise to his ears. A giggle went around the room. *Say no!* he was thinking, but his lips wouldn't move. Maybe if he refused Caroline as a partner, the teacher would flunk him before he even began.

"Well, we hadn't quite got to that, Caroline, but I'll put it down," Miss Applebaum said, and made a note in her planning book.

Wally swallowed. Any minute he expected to feel Caroline's breath on the back of his neck, Caroline's pen poking his shoulder. Nothing happened, however, and he listened as Miss Applebaum explained what the December project was.

"We're going to work on improving our listening, observing, and writing skills," she explained. "Writers will tell you that only a small part of what they do is actually putting words on paper. Most of their time is spent paying attention to what is going on around them, imagining themselves in the place of their characters."

Wally began to feel sick.

"What I want you to do, after you have chosen partners, is to interview each other. Find out everything you can about your partners—what they like to eat, to read, to watch on TV, to do. And then, for a whole day, I want you to try to live as if you really were your partners, eating what they eat, doing what they like to do. The report you will write for me will be in two parts: part one, your interview with your partner, what you have found out about him or her; and part two, how it feels to 'be' that person for a day, the ways in which you're alike and the ways you're different. We have an even number of students in class, so no one should be left out. You may choose your partners now."

Everyone began talking, calling across the room, friends calling friends, laughter, shouts.

Not Wally. Wally Hatford sat face forward, eyes on the blackboard, wondering what would happen if he just went down to the Greyhound bus depot, bought a ticket to anywhere, and didn't come back till Christmas.

He had to interview Caroline Malloy?

He had to let *her* interview *him*?—to ask questions about what he liked, how he lived, what he *ate*?

And then, as though that weren't enough, he had to *be* Caroline for a day? Did Miss Applebaum go to Torture School to come up with these projects or did she think them up all by herself in the dead of night?

11

"Oh, Wal-ly!" teased one of his friends in the next row. "How's it going to feel to be Car-o-line?"

"Yeah, where are you going to go for your *interview*?" asked a girl, giggling.

But Wally was surprised to hear Caroline say, "We're going to interview like everybody else, and there's nothing silly about it."

He could hardly believe his ears. She still sounded polite. She sounded grown-up, yet she was a year younger than he was. She sounded, in fact, perfectly normal.

Still, he did not want to be Caroline Malloy for a day. He did not want to be her for even a minute, and he did not want her to be him. He could have chosen Bill Thompkins or Bobby Lister or John Meese—*anyone* but Caroline.

He did not sit at her table at lunchtime.

He did not go near her at recess.

"Hey, Wally, I hear you've got a girlfriend," his buddies teased when they came back inside for class.

And one of the girls called, "Caroline Malloy thinks you're cute!"

Wally felt like throwing up. He was not cute. He was not a boyfriend, and Miss Applebaum's December project was one of the dumbest assignments he'd ever had.

After school he waited outside for Peter, who was carrying a school bag with purple dinosaurs on it, and then Jake and Josh, who were wearing baseball caps backward, and the four of them started the walk home along the Buckman River.

"What's up?" Josh asked Wally.

"I don't want to talk about it," said Wally, staring at the water and thinking how, if it weren't for the river, Caroline Malloy would be living even closer to him than she did now. How could it be that he had been feeling so good when he started off to school that morning, and so awful now?

"Why? What happened?" asked Jake.

"I have to be Caroline Malloy for a day and she has to be me," said Wally.

"You have to wear her clothes and everything?" Peter asked.

"No!" yelped Wally. But he told his brothers how he had to interview her and do whatever she would do for a day. "Worst of all," he said, "she chose me for a partner in front of the whole class, and now kids are saying I'm her boyfriend."

"Ha!" said Jake. "That's easy to fix."

"*How?* I've got to do this, Jake! I can't say no. If we don't do our December projects, we practically flunk fourth grade!"

"So *do* it," said Jake. "If you have to be her for a day, she has to be you, doesn't she?" Jake was beginning to grin.

"Yes," said Wally.

"She has to do whatever you tell her you'd be doing?" added Josh.

"Yes . . . ," said Wally. And then the light began to dawn. It was a wonderful thought. A wonderful, terrible thought. He would tell Caroline Malloy that he loved to do something he knew she would hate. That he loved to eat things that would gross her out. Wally began to smile.

It made him feel a little bad, because Caroline had been especially nice to him lately. But what if there was a January project and a February project, and Caroline chose him for a partner every time? If the Malloys didn't go back to Ohio at the end of the summer, there might be fifth- and sixth-grade projects as well, and then she'd follow him into junior high school and high school and . . .

"Only nine more months and the Bensons come back," said Jake, saying what they all were thinking.

"We hope," added Josh. But strangely, Wally noticed, he didn't sound all that eager.

■ ■ ■ ■ ■ ■ ■ ■ ■ ■ ■

# Three

■

# The Promise

"You look awfully smug," Beth said to Caroline at dinner that evening.

"I do?" Caroline looked innocently around the table. "I was thinking about school, actually. I'm doing a special project with Wally Hatford."

"Well, that's a change!" said Mother. "I'm glad to see you getting along with the Hatfords, dear. They seem like such nice people."

Eddie put one hand over her mouth and gagged, but Caroline was surprised to hear Beth say, "I think Josh is the nicest. You should see his paintings, Mother. One hall at school is decorated with student paintings, and four of them were done by Josh."

"Airplanes, mostly," said Eddie. "Airplanes and horses and cars."

"But they're good!" said Beth.

"My, haven't *we* changed!" said Eddie.

Eddie too, however, seemed to have other things on

her mind besides teasing the boys. Though she had never been advanced a grade as Caroline had, she was considered the brain of the family, and she often had other things on her mind besides softball. "I think I've decided what I want to do when I'm grown," she announced, examining a stalk of broccoli before she popped it into her mouth.

Father looked up, fork poised. "Yes?" he said.

"Sports medicine. Treat athletes."

"Ouch!" said Coach Malloy.

"*What?*" asked Eddie.

"That was my wallet groaning," said Dad. "A sports doctor means medical school, you know."

"I know," said Eddie. "But I think I'd be good at it. I'm good in science."

"You *would* be good at it, Eddie, and if that's what you want, we'll see you through school," her father told her.

"I think that would be a wonderful career for you," Mother said, looking at Eddie admiringly.

Caroline pushed her meat loaf from one side of her plate to the other. There went her dream of a Malloy movie studio. But she could still be a stage actress.

"Well, I know what *I* want to be too," she told her parents. "An actress on Broadway."

"Caroline, you're always onstage, twenty-four hours a day," said her father. "You can't even tie your shoes without making a production of it."

Caroline wasn't sure if that was a compliment or not. Miss Applebaum, though, had said that writing was only part of being a writer—the rest was observing and listening. Maybe the same was true of an

16

actress. You were always practicing, making a story out of the everyday things that happened to you.

"When do you have to decide what you want to be?" asked Beth. "I haven't the slightest idea what *I'll* do."

"Hopefully, before you're through college," her father said.

Caroline curled up in a chair in the living room after dinner and wrote out a list of questions she was going to ask Wally. She was certainly being friendly enough to him—even choosing him for her partner. He would just *have* to open any present she gave him!

*What is your favorite food?*
*What is your favorite game?*
*What is your favorite TV show?*
*What kind of books do you like to read?*
*What time do you go to bed?*
*What time do you get up?*

She was thinking about what she would put in her report. Then she started thinking about how she would *give* the report. That was even better. Whenever Caroline had to stand up in front of the class and read something, it was her favorite time of day. And for the second time that week, she had a wonderful idea. An awful idea. A wonderful, awful idea, and she gave up all thought of being kind to Wally. This idea was too good to let go.

If she could slip into the rest room just before it was time to give her report and actually put on Wally's clothes, she would get an A+++ on her report.

How could Miss Applebaum *not* give her the best grade in class? She would even *look* like Wally. But she knew as sure as she had eyes in her head that Wally would never lend her any of his clothes.

That Saturday, Caroline went to the five-and-dime to buy some socks and saw seven-year-old Peter. He was standing at the Matchbox car display case, turning it around and around and saying to himself, "I've got that one . . . don't have that one . . . I've got that one . . . don't have that one . . ."

"Hi, Peter," she said.

"Hi, Caroline," said Peter, and he gave her a big smile, showing a missing tooth on both the top and the bottom. He was on the short side, a little chubby, and had an adorable smile.

"How many Matchbox cars do you have?" she asked him, her mind racing on ahead of her.

"Seventeen," Peter said.

"If you could have any car you wanted, which one would you choose?"

Peter slowly turned the display case some more until he came to a red double-decker tour bus. "That one," he said.

Caroline looked at the price. She mentally counted out the money she had in her bank back home, and the money she had in her pocket.

"I'll buy it for you if you'll make a deal," Caroline said.

Peter's eyes opened wide.

"Come on down the street with me to the drugstore and we'll talk about it over a fudge sundae," Caroline told him.

"O-*kay*!" said Peter, smiling even wider.

"A *hot* fudge sundae," Caroline said as they stepped outside and into a cloud of snowflakes.

Peter skipped happily alongside her, reciting the names of the seventeen Matchbox cars in his collection. At the drugstore they took a booth, and Caroline ordered one sundae and two spoons.

"Now listen carefully, Peter," she said. "Because if I'm going to buy you that double-decker bus, you've got to do something for me, and you've got to keep it secret. That's the important part."

Peter looked a little worried. "Is it bad? Will I get in trouble?"

"I don't think it's bad, and if it's not bad, I don't see how you can get in trouble," Caroline told him.

The sundae came with a little pitcher of thick hot fudge sauce to pour over it, and they took turns with their spoons. Caroline even let Peter have the first bite.

"First of all," said Caroline, "you've got to promise—cross your heart and hope to die, Peter—that you won't tell *anybody* until it's over. Then you can tell the whole world. But for now you have to keep it secret."

Peter paused, then looked at the big spoonful of chocolate he was digging up, and nodded.

"Okay, here's the deal. Wally and I are partners in a project at school, and we have to sort of be each other for a day."

"I know," said Peter. "He already told me. Only he doesn't want to wear your clothes."

"I wouldn't want him to, but *I* want to wear *his*.

19

Just for one day. And it's got to be a surprise, so what I want you to do, without telling anyone, is to bring me a set of Wally's clothes—shirt, pants, socks, shoes, cap—that I can wear just long enough to give my report at school, and then I'll give them back. But you can't let anyone see you take them, or tell anybody what you've done until it's over. If you do, you don't get the double-decker bus."

"Wally'll be mad," said Peter.

"It's only for a little while. You won't want to take his best clothes, though, because he'd miss them. Bring me stuff he doesn't wear too often. You can give them to me a little at a time if you like, but I've got to have them by next week. And as soon as I have a whole set to wear, I'll go back to the five-and-dime and buy you that bus. Deal?"

"Deal," said Peter.

"Shake?" Caroline put out her hand.

"Shake," said Peter.

Caroline slid the dish over to Peter's side of the table and let him finish the sundae. Actresses had to do all kinds of things to get the right part, she thought.

She imagined going to school with Wally's clothes in a paper bag. She imagined slipping off to the rest room just before she gave her report. She imagined Wally Hatford's face when she stood up in front of the class wearing his shirt, his pants, his socks, his shoes.

Caroline was smiling. She couldn't help it.

" ' 'Tis the season to be jolly . . . !' " she sang as she made her way back home.

# Four

■

# Phone Call

Wally was making up a list of things to ask Caroline. The problem was, he was finding out more about her than he wanted to know. He didn't really *care* what her favorite foods were or whether she liked mysteries more than science fiction. But he had to fill up at least two pages, according to Miss Applebaum, so he continued to write:

> *What's the latest time you ever went to bed?*
> *Have you ever broken any bones?*
> *Which do you hate most—going to the dentist or throwing up?*

Wally lay on his stomach with a pencil and a pad of paper. He caught some movement out of the corner of his eye, and looked over to see Peter picking something up from the floor and stuffing it into his pocket.

"What are you doing with my underpants?" Wally asked, rising up on one elbow.

Peter paused, like a boy caught with his hand in the cookie jar. "Oh!" he said. "Are these *your* underpants?"

"They were on my floor, weren't they? Yours have Batman all over them, mine are plain. Put them back."

Wally went on writing on his notepad: *Did you ever find any shark's teeth?*

This time he heard a noise behind him. Wally turned to see Peter trying to sneak a pair of socks out of his drawer.

"What are you *doing*? Put them back!" he insisted.

"I—I just wanted to see if you had any of my socks," said Peter.

"What do you mean? Why would I have your socks? Get out of here!" Wally said. *Jeez, what a weird brother!*

Peter left.

From his bedroom window, Wally could see the Buckman River, which looped around the end of Island Avenue and came flowing back again on the other side. A road bridge linked the people on Island Avenue with downtown, but there was an old swinging bridge near the Hatfords' place that provided a shortcut for pedestrians. It was across this bridge that the Malloy girls walked to school every morning, and it was this bridge that the Hatford boys used to cross when the Bensons lived in the big house where the Malloys were now.

Wally liked Buckman. He liked the city hall, Murphy's Five and Dime, Larkin's Pharmacy with its soda fountain and marble-topped tables, Oldakers' Bookstore with the trapdoor leading to the cellar. He liked the river and the swinging bridge. He liked the way things used to be when the Bensons were here.

If the Bensons lived here now, Wally Hatford wouldn't be lying on his bed on a Saturday morning thinking up questions to ask a girl. First of all, he and Bill Benson would be project partners. He and his brothers and the five Benson brothers might be downstairs at the dining room table starting a game of Monopoly that would last all day. They might be setting out to hike along the river or explore Smuggler's Cove. They might be looking for Indian arrowheads up in the meadow or fooling around the old coal mine.

"Put nine boys together, and they can always think up something to do," Mom used to say.

"Put nine boys together, and you've got a baseball team," Dad had answered.

Now, half the team was down in Georgia, and Eddie Malloy, across the river, was determined to make the Buckman Elementary School softball team come spring.

Wally sighed and rolled over on his back. He'd better get this job finished fast because he still had Christmas presents to buy for the family, and he hadn't even started. Right this very minute Josh was across the hall painting a picture for Mom from an old photograph of a windmill. Mom loved handmade presents. But what was Wally doing? Trying to guess how far the beam of sunlight on the opposite wall would travel before the sun disappeared over the roof.

The phone rang downstairs. Mom was working at the hardware store, and Dad was delivering mail, so Wally was about to get up and answer when he heard Josh come out of his room and pick up the receiver.

"Hello? . . . Hey! How you doin'?" Josh said. "Jake! Wally! It's the Bensons! They're calling from Georgia. Get on the other phone, you guys."

There were only two phones in the house, so Wally had to share the upstairs phone with Josh while Jake and Peter picked up the telephone downstairs.

"We were just wondering if it had snowed yet up there," Bill Benson said. "Man, that's one thing we're going to miss this Christmas. Snow."

Wally and Josh gave each other a high five. It was the first time since the Bensons had moved away that they'd really sounded as though they were missing Buckman. All they'd talked about so far was all the fun things they were doing in their new town, and about Danny's teacher, whom they called a "Georgia peach."

"It hasn't snowed much yet, but it feels like it's going to," Jake said from downstairs.

"Yeah, you guys come back here when it snows and we'll have the biggest snowball fight in history," said Wally into the phone.

They talked a few minutes about school, and then one of the Benson boys asked, "So how are those weirdos over at our place?"

"Weird as ever," said Jake. "I don't know, they've been sort of quiet lately. I'm not sure what they're up to."

"You ought to rig up some way to spy on them," Tony Benson said. "You know that window up in the loft of our old garage? Remember when we used to hold club meetings up there? You could see right into our upstairs windows."

"Yeah, but how do we walk into your garage now and say we want to use the loft?" asked Josh.

"Easy," said Bill Benson. "Just say . . . say that when we moved we gave you guys rights to hold club meetings there."

"How can we do that?" asked Wally.

"Haven't you ever heard of squatters' rights? It means when somebody has been using property for a long time, whether he owns it or not, if nobody has kicked him out, then he has certain rights to it. Tell them the club is still going on, and you guys want to keep meeting in the same place. Then take your binoculars up there and see what the girls are up to."

Josh began to grin, but Wally felt a little sick. He wanted *less* to do with the Malloy sisters, not more.

"Besides," said Steve Benson, "Coach and Mrs. Malloy won't care. What do they use the loft for? Nothing, I'll bet."

"But . . . but what kind of a club are we supposed to say it is?" asked Wally. "We never even had a name for it."

"A pizza club," Peter suggested. "We could crawl up there and eat pizza."

"Don't be dumb," Wally heard Jake say from downstairs. "We could eat pizza at home. It should be something we do outside."

"What about an astronomy club?" asked another Benson. "You could be studying the stars from the loft window."

"Huh-uh," said Jake. "We could climb up on our own roof to do that."

He was right, Wally thought. The Hatford house had a tiny little porch on top, called a widow's walk, that you reached through a trapdoor in the attic ceiling. Widows' walks used to be built on old houses near the sea, so that wives could go up there and look for their husbands' ships returning home, only sometimes the ships never made it, and then the wives became widows. Why someone built a widow's walk overlooking the Buckman River, where the water at its deepest was six feet, Wally never did understand.

"I know!" Josh said finally. "Let's call it the Explorers' Club. That could be almost anything."

"Yeah," said Peter. "We're explorers."

"Why don't you guys send us something official-looking to show to the weirdos, to prove we get to use the loft?" said Jake.

"All right," Bill promised. "I'll type it up on the computer and send it by e-mail."

When the Bensons hung up, Wally and Josh went downstairs, and all four boys rummaged about the kitchen looking for crackers and peanut butter. Josh and Jake were as long and lean as pretzel sticks, but still they were always hungry. They talked some about Christmas, and Wally was dismayed to discover that

Jake had been working on a present too: He had bought a little plastic cabinet with tiny drawers in it for Dad, and was going to sort out all Dad's nuts and bolts and screws and nails and fill up the drawers. It was something Bill Benson had once given *his* father for Christmas.

"Man, I miss the Bensons," Jake said, smearing one of the crackers heavily with peanut butter and popping it into his mouth. "I sure wish they'd move back."

There was quiet around the table for a minute or two, broken only by the sound of munching.

"Think of all the fun we could have if the Bensons came back and we teased the Malloy girls together!" Josh suggested.

"If the Bensons come back, the Malloys go back to Ohio, remember?" said Wally.

"Maybe they won't. Maybe the Bensons will come back and the Malloys will decide to stay too, just move to another house," said Josh.

"Yeah!" said Peter. "Then we could *all* live in Buckman."

Peter sounded a little too eager, Wally thought. Living in the same town as the Malloy sisters was like having cats and dogs in the same pen. It was like trying to mix oil and water. It just didn't work.

# Five

■

# Company

So far, all Caroline had managed to get from Peter was one of Wally's old T-shirts with BUCKMAN EXXON on it in red-and-blue letters. She would rather have had a T-shirt with the word WALLY across the front, but Wally wore the Exxon shirt so much that everyone would know it was his when she put it on. Of course, she had to wash it first. It smelled like sweat and peanut butter.

"Keep trying," she told Peter. "You don't get the double-decker Matchbox bus till I get his shoes and pants too."

At school, when the first reports were being read in class, Miss Applebaum did not seem especially pleased with them.

"Students, listen," she said. "A good interviewer does not just ask yes-or-no questions. The interviewer's job is to get a person talking about things that interest him. If he says he doesn't like school or he doesn't like sports, ask why. If he says history is his favorite subject, ask why. A one-word answer means that the question wasn't any good."

Caroline saw Wally Hatford's shoulders rise in despair and heard a small sigh come from his chest. They had already agreed to meet at the library on Saturday and interview each other across a reading table. She smiled to herself. No matter what Wally did, her report would be better than his because she would be standing in front of the class wearing his clothes!

Meanwhile, Christmas lights were coming on all over Buckman. Christmas bells and greenery decorated all the lampposts on Main Street. Oldakers' Bookstore had Christmas picture books and teddy bears in the window. The five-and-dime had a display of Christmas ornaments, and the hardware store was featuring sleds and snow saucers.

Mrs. Malloy came home one afternoon with some blue crinkle ribbon and a huge roll of wrapping paper decorated with blue-and-gold angels.

"I found these on sale at the hardware store," she said. "You hardly ever find Christmas wrap on sale before Christmas, but Mrs. Hatford told me about it when I went in to buy a tree stand. We could wrap all our presents in angel paper this year."

"I need to get my secretary a present," Coach Malloy told her. "If you get any ideas, let me know. I haven't known her long enough to guess what she likes."

"What *I* would like for Christmas is to go back to Ohio," said Eddie. "There isn't any girls' softball team here, and if I don't make the boys' team next spring, I won't be playing at all."

"Well, don't give up yet," said her father. "When they see how you can hit, Eddie, I have a feeling they'll take you on."

"And I haven't heard anything about a science fair, either," Eddie continued. "I had a special experiment I wanted to do this time on photosynthesis."

"Just wait and see what happens," said Mother. "The school year isn't even half over."

"Are we going to invite the Hatfords for Christmas dinner?" asked Beth.

Mrs. Malloy looked surprised. "Why, no, I hadn't planned on it. Why? Do you think I should?"

Beth shrugged. "I don't know. They invited us for Thanksgiving. I thought maybe we'd be inviting them for Christmas."

Caroline gave her sister an *Are you crazy?* look. The Hatfords? *Here?* At *Christmas?*

"Well, maybe I could invite them over for cookies and punch one evening during Christmas week," Mother continued. "There's just so much going on, though—the college is having a faculty party and there are all the Christmas concerts . . ."

Caroline thought of the gross-me-out present she was preparing for Wally. She still didn't know what it would be, but she knew it would be awful. Having the Hatfords there at Christmas was *not* a good idea.

"I don't think we need to do that, Mother," she said.

"Yeah," said Eddie. "Let's just send them a card."

"Well, we'll see," Mother replied.

Saturday came, and Caroline put on her parka, picked up her notebook, and walked to the library. As she was going up the steps, she could see that Wally was there ahead of her. He was standing just inside the door with his hands in the pockets of his jacket, looking around uncomfortably.

Caroline could not resist. She softly pushed the door open, stepped up behind Wally, and poked him in the back with the corner of her notebook.

Wally wheeled around.

"Hi," she said. "You want to sit down at a table over there and ask each other our questions?" He nodded, so she led the way to a table in the corner. She took off her parka and gloves, but Wally left his on and sat in the chair sideways, as though ready to bolt from the room at any minute.

"You want to ask yours first, or what?" said Caroline.

"I don't care," said Wally.

Caroline tried to be as polite as possible. "Okay, you first," she told him, and leaned back with her hands in her lap.

Wally reached into his pocket and took out a piece of paper folded into eight sections. He slowly unfolded it, cleared his throat, scratched his head, and said, "Would you rather go to the dentist or throw up?"

*Good grief,* thought Caroline, as the minutes ticked by. How was he supposed to be her for a day if he didn't ask any better questions than that? Maybe that was the point, she decided. He didn't *want* to do anything different at all, so he was careful about what he asked.

But when it was her turn to interview Wally, Caroline got the shock of her life.

"What's your favorite food?" she asked.

"Parsnips and chicken livers," Wally said, and Caroline was sure he was trying not to laugh.

"Favorite book?" she asked.

"*The History of Military Strategy in the United States in the Eighteenth Century,*" he told her. He must have seen that title on a library shelf, Caroline decided, the most boring book he could find, just so she'd have to read it.

Favorite music? *Violin concertos.*

Favorite TV program? *Wall Street Week.*

Caroline didn't think she could stand it.

"You're making this up just so I'll have to do it!" she said.

"How do you know? You don't live at my house," Wally told her.

"Wally, you've never read a book like that in your life!" Caroline protested.

"I *love* military strategy," he said, grinning.

Caroline tried hard to keep her temper, but they could never be friends in a million years, she decided. She and Wally Hatford just didn't mix.

The following day, the Malloys were enjoying a Sunday afternoon at home. Beth and Eddie were in the kitchen helping Mother bake Christmas cookies; Coach Malloy, who taught chemistry too, was grading papers on one side of the dining room table; Caroline was on the other side writing up her report.

The doorbell rang.

"Somebody else will have to get that," Mother called from the kitchen. "We're just taking a batch of cookies out of the oven."

"I'll get it," said Caroline's father.

He put down his pen and walked to the front door.

"Well, hello there," Caroline heard him say. "Come in!"

She looked up to see the four Hatford brothers walk into the hallway. Jake was holding a piece of paper, and Caroline thought they looked somewhat nervous.

"Who is it?" called Mother.

"The Hatford boys," said the coach.

At that, Beth and Eddie emerged from the kitchen. Beth still had a hot pad in her hand.

"Well, I have some cookies for them," Mother called. "Tell them to have a seat."

"Sit down! Sit down!" said Caroline's father.

In the dining room, Caroline put down her pencil and watched. Now what was all this about? she wondered.

"We can't stay very long," said Josh.

"We're always glad to have you visit," said Coach Malloy. "Beth? Eddie? You girls and Caroline come in here and say hello. We've got company."

Eddie came into the living room and stood leaning against the doorway. Beth put down the hot pad and sat on the hassock next to the fireplace. Caroline stayed right where she was because she could see the whole room.

"We just thought maybe we ought to show you this

paper we got from the Bensons," Josh said. "I mean, to make it official and everything."

. "What's this?" asked Coach Malloy. He pulled his glasses back out of his pocket and stuck them on again.

"Well, your garage used to be our clubhouse. I mean, we were up there in the loft a lot before the Bensons moved to Georgia," Jake tried to explain.

"Yeah. The Explorers' Club!" put in Peter.

"And . . . we'd like to keep on meeting there, if it's okay with you," said Josh.

"Squatters' rights," said Wally.

Coach Malloy took the paper and looked it over. He smiled just a little.

"Squatters' rights, huh?" he said. "All you want to do is meet in the garage? Well, I certainly have no objection to that, boys. And if you ever want to wash my car while you're in there, go right ahead."

"Wait a minute!" said Eddie. "Those guys are going to be up there in our loft?"

"The Bensons' loft," Jake corrected.

"We're explorers," said Peter importantly.

"Yeah, and I'm the tooth fairy," said Eddie. "Dad, you don't know what you're doing! Trust me!"

But Coach Malloy only laughed, and invited the boys to have a snack.

■ ■ ■ ■ ■ ■ ■ ■ ■ ■ ■

# Six

■

## Class Report

"**D**id you see the look on Eddie's face when her dad said we could meet in their loft?" Jake chortled as the boys went back across the swinging bridge, their pockets full of Christmas cookies. "She would have clobbered us if she could."

Jake was usually the mastermind behind whatever plot the Hatfords hatched. He had been the first of the twins to be born, and he "just seemed to go right on leading the way," Mother always said.

Josh was quieter. Where Jake liked to be doing something, Josh liked to make things. There wasn't another person in the whole family who could draw a straight line, but Josh had enough talent to make up for it.

The bridge swayed and bounced with every step they took. Peter was the only one who still held on to the cable handrail as he crossed.

"Yeah, Caroline freaked out too," said Wally. "Did you see the way she put her head down on the table?"

"They make good cookies, though," said Peter, chewing noisily.

The only one who hadn't said anything so far was Josh, and when they reached the other side of the river, he said, "Beth didn't seem to mind much."

"She didn't?" asked Wally. "She *wants* us to spy on her?"

"She doesn't even know we're going to spy," said Josh. "She just . . . didn't seem too surprised, I guess. I don't know. I think she's nicer than Eddie or Caroline."

"How do you figure that?" asked Jake.

"She just is. She doesn't yell at us like Eddie does."

"She's prettier, too!" put in Peter.

"Ha! You turn your back on any one of those girls and no telling what would happen," said Jake. "At least this way we'll be able to see what they're up to."

When they got home, their father was putting up the Christmas tree, and suddenly the Malloy girls were forgotten. Everybody had a turn saying whether the tree should lean a little more to the left or the right, and finally it was secure in its stand, its top almost touching the ceiling.

"You guys bring down the ornaments from the attic, now, and help your mother with the decorating," Dad said. "With all the extra holiday mail, I'm working late every day from now till Christmas, and I'm beat." He sprawled out in a chair and took off his shoes.

"We will," said Josh, and the boys scrambled up the stairs to the attic.

Finally, when the living room floor was covered with boxes, Mrs. Hatford brought in a bowl of popcorn and set it on the coffee table. "I thought maybe we'd like a snack while we decorate the tree," she said.

"Why don't we ever have cookies?" asked Peter. "The kind that look like bells and stars, and have sparkles and frosting on them?"

"Because I work at the hardware store, Peter, and I'm simply too tired to bake in the evenings," Mother said.

"Popcorn is fine," Wally told her, full of the Christmas spirit, and he set to work stringing the lights. In fact, he was feeling particularly good. He had managed not to ask Caroline Malloy one single question that would require him to do anything different to live as she did for one day. Get up, eat breakfast, go to school, come home—that was it.

On the other hand, she was going to have to do all kinds of dumb stuff if she did what he had told her *he* liked to do. Not only that, but he and his brothers got to use the Bensons' loft while they were away.

It wasn't that he hated the Malloy sisters. He didn't even dislike them, really. He just wished that Caroline would leave him alone. Caroline nice was almost as scary as Caroline mean. He just wanted them to stay on their side of the river and he would stay on his, that's all. But as long as Caroline kept poking her nose in his business, he would poke his nose in hers.

When Mother got out the little white reindeer with

the red bows around their necks, she said, "I met Mrs. Malloy in the supermarket last night, and she said the strangest thing. She seemed to think I had a gourmet recipe for parsnips and chicken livers, and wondered if she could borrow it. She said Caroline needed to try it. Isn't that strange? It sounds perfectly awful to me."

Wally, who had picked up a handful of tinsel, felt it fall through his fingers again. "What . . . did you tell her?" he asked.

"I said it sounded positively disgusting. That we never ate parsnips and didn't much care for chicken livers either. She said that Caroline must have misunderstood. 'I guess she did!' I told her. 'The favorite food in our house is pizza.' Then Caroline came by the hardware store and said she was looking for a book called *Military Strategy* . . . oh, I forget the exact title. It wasn't in the library, and she wondered if we had a copy."

Wally's voice began to squeak. "What did you tell her?" he asked again.

"I told her it was not a book that anyone in our family would read, and she'd better try someone else. Then she said she was looking for a good book to read herself, and wondered what your favorite books were, Wally. I told her about those mysteries on your shelf and she thanked me and said it was exactly the kind of book she wanted, and maybe she'd come over and borrow one sometime. I hope I said the right thing— that she was welcome to borrow one of yours."

Wally held back a groan.

"She even asked what time you went to bed, and I told her as late as you possibly could—that more than

38

once I'd found you reading by flashlight under the blankets. Is that girl sweet on you or something—all these questions?"

This time a long tortured cry came from Wally's lips.

"Mom, I wish you wouldn't talk about me to Caroline. I don't care what she asks, you don't have to tell her."

Mrs. Hatford looked confused. "I didn't know what else to do, Wally. She's obviously interested in you. She was just being nice."

"She wasn't being nice, Mom, she was being nosy! The next time Caroline asks you a question, tell her to ask me."

"All right," said his mother. "Why do I get the feeling that I don't know half of what goes on around here?"

"Because you probably don't, Ellen," said her husband. "And I have the feeling you wouldn't want to know. Let Wally and Caroline work things out for themselves."

*Great!* thought Wally. Now Caroline not only had proof that he was fibbing, but she had the correct answers too. Now she got to eat pizza and stay up late and read mystery books too!

■

Wally dreaded going to school on Monday because they had to give their reports on each other, and he hadn't spent very much time trying to imagine what it would feel like to be Caroline. In fact, he hadn't tried to imagine it at all.

He got out of bed at last, and looked for his baggy

blue pants. He couldn't find them anywhere. He put on a pair of old jeans instead, and then he looked for his sneakers with the purple laces. He couldn't find those either.

Wally stood in the center of his floor, tipped back his head, and bellowed at the ceiling, one long, continuous *"Arrrggghhh!"*

"You calling a moose?" asked his father, sticking his head in the bedroom. "Hurry and dress, now. If you're ready when I leave for the P.O., I'll give you a ride. It's cold out there."

The four boys ate their cereal, then piled into Dad's car. Peter was lugging a big plastic leaf bag, which he clutched tightly in one hand, and was the first out of the car when they reached the school. He ran on ahead of the others and disappeared down a corridor toward his second-grade class.

After Miss Applebaum had taken the roll, she said, "We still have eight more reports to hear, so I think we'll start with those this morning. I want to finish them before Christmas vacation. Remember, I'm looking for how well we are increasing our powers of observation. I want to see how well you listened, how original you were with your questions, and what you learned about the art of the interview. Wally and Caroline, you're next on my list. Who wants to go first?"

"I do," said Wally. He wanted to get it over with. He wanted to feel that this would be the last time in his entire life he would ever have to say Caroline's name out loud in public.

He stood up in front of the room and tried not to look at Caroline. He told the class when Caroline was born, and how she'd had the chicken pox but not the mumps. She had two fillings in her teeth, she'd never broken a bone, and she would rather go to the dentist than throw up. "What was it like to be Caroline Malloy for a day?" he said. "Actually, rather boring," he answered. And then he sat down. He heard Caroline asking permission to go to the rest room, and her footsteps leaving the room. *Ha!* He grinned in spite of himself.

Miss Applebaum was frowning, however. She said that while the questions Wally had asked Caroline might have seemed original, they did not deal with the important things about a person at all, and therefore we did not know Caroline much better after the interview than we did before.

Wally didn't care. *Flunk me,* he decided. It would be worth it just to make sure he wouldn't have to be in Caroline's class next year if the Malloys stayed on.

As the class discussed what was good about his report and what wasn't, Wally realized suddenly that there was no one breathing on the back of his neck, no poke in the ribs. Caroline wasn't back yet. What was taking her so long? Had she gone home?

"All right, let's hear from Caroline next," Miss Applebaum said, and then she asked, "Where *is* Caroline?" The door at the back of the room opened, and in walked Caroline Malloy.

She had on a T-shirt that said BUCKMAN EXXON in red-and-blue letters on the front, baggy blue pants, white tube socks with yellow and green stripes around the tops (she'd rolled the pant legs up so everyone could see), a pair of black Nikes with purple laces, and a dirty baseball cap worn backward. Everyone started to laugh.

"What it feels like to be Wally Hatford," Caroline began, smiling too. She patted the clothes she was wearing: "Wally's shirt, Wally's trousers, Wally's socks . . ." She held up one foot. "Wally's shoes . . ." And then, most humiliating of all, Wally found, she raised the bottom of the T-shirt to show the waistband of his Fruit Of The Looms: "Wally's underpants."

# Seven

■

# Humiliation

Caroline was in her glory. The only thing better than this would be standing onstage in a huge auditorium before a thousand people.

She loved being onstage. She *adored* being the center of attention. And someday, she knew, her name would be in lights on Broadway and people would pay a hundred dollars just to see Caroline Lenore Malloy in a play.

Meanwhile, she had to make do with the fourth-grade class at Buckman Elementary, and she played it for all it was worth.

"I decided that if I had to be Wally Hatford for a day, I should be as close to the real thing as I could get, so I borrowed his clothes," she said.

The class laughed again, and Caroline could see Wally's ears burning as red as the nose on Rudolph the Reindeer.

*It serves him right,* she told herself. Wally could describe her as dramatic or loud or conceited or even crazy, but how dare he call her boring? Caroline Malloy was never boring. And so the brighter Wally's ears burned, the better she felt.

"What it's like to be Wally Hatford for a day is to be Mr. Average," she continued. "He isn't very smart, but you can't call him stupid; he's never late for school, but he takes his time about getting here. The most interesting feature about Wallace James Hatford is that he lies."

Miss Applebaum leaned forward and looked at Caroline. Caroline merely nodded for emphasis.

"It's sad, but true. I discovered later that everything he told me during our interview was a lie. His favorite food is not parsnips and chicken livers, it's pizza. The best book he ever read was not *The History of Military Strategy in the United States in the Eighteenth Century,* it's *The Bodies in the Bessledorf Hotel.* It took some skillful detective work on my part, but I—"

"May I interrupt?" came Miss Applebaum's voice from behind her.

Caroline frowned as she turned toward the teacher's desk. *How rude!* Whoever heard of interrupting an actress during a play! *Stay in character,* she told herself. *Just freeze, and as soon as she stops talking, start in again right where you left off.* This would be a good lesson in improvising.

"Class," said Miss Applebaum. "These two reports are the finest examples I know of how *not* to conduct an interview. Caroline and Wally were obviously more intent on annoying each other than they were in doing this assignment, which was to improve our observing and listening skills. An interviewer who approaches her subject already knowing how she feels about him cannot possibly be unprejudiced. An interview like that is worse than no interview at all, because it simply passes on to others our own prejudices. Therefore, both Wally and Caroline have failed the December project, and I don't think we need to hear any more, Caroline. You may take your seat."

Caroline stood speechless at the front of the room. This couldn't be happening! You simply did not turn off the lights in the middle of a performance! You did not pull the curtain when the actress was center stage. She still had her best lines to say! She still had to tell how Wally—

"You may sit down, Caroline," the teacher said again. "Though I would suggest you go into the rest room and change back into your own clothes."

It was Caroline's face that burned now, but Wally seemed to take no pleasure in it. His ears were still fiery red and he sat staring down at a pencil eraser on his desk.

The rest of the class watched as Caroline stumbled back to her seat, picked up the shopping bag with her own clothes in it, and fled the room, tears running down her cheeks.

This was horrible! It was awful! She had heard of plays closing in New York after only a few performances, but she had never, ever heard of a play so bad that they brought down the curtain right in the middle of the show. She leaned against the paper-towel dispenser and bawled.

For the rest of the day Caroline did not look at

Wally or he at her. She hardly looked at anyone else either, and the other kids left her alone. How would she ever get over the embarrassment? She would never live it down—never, never, never! Why hadn't Miss Applebaum sent Wally to his seat when he described her as boring? He had deserved everything she'd said about him! And then, silently interviewing herself, Caroline admitted that she had planned the grand humiliation of Wally Hatford even before he'd got up to give his report. Even before he'd called her life boring. In fact, the only reason she'd chosen him for a partner at all was to make him think she was his friend so he would accept a gross-me-out present.

How could she think he would be friendly now? How did she think he'd dare open any gift she gave him? She had gotten so carried away by her own plans that she'd forgotten what she'd set out to do in the first place.

*I don't care,* she thought angrily, turning all her anger back onto Wally again. *I am going to make him as miserable as I can this Christmas, and if we're both stuck in fourth grade for the rest of our lives, he'll be sorry he ever heard the name Malloy.*

Miss Applebaum did not say anything more to either Caroline or Wally that afternoon. The fact that it was snowing when school let out made it even worse somehow. Ordinarily, Caroline would climb up on the highest object handy, toss back her head, throw out her arms, and cry, "Snow! Wonderful snow!", letting it coat her hair and eyelashes.

But she shuffled along with her head down, her

shoulders hunched, until Beth caught up with her and grabbed her arm.

"Caroline, what's wrong?" she asked.

Caroline was afraid to answer for fear she might cry again. And if she cried out here on the sidewalk, someone would be bound to see and report it to the Hatfords. How could she feel so miserable in the season of peace and joy? How could she have *acted* so miserable, even to Wally Hatford?

"What's wrong?" Beth asked again.

"Only the major embarrassment of my life," Caroline replied, choking. "Not only that, but I—I failed fourth grade!" Her tears came in spite of herself. But by then Eddie had caught up with them, and, comforted by the presence of her two older sisters, one on either side of her, Caroline spilled out her story in gulps and sniffles.

"Yikes!" said Beth. "Major, major embarrassment!"

"It was a stupid, stupid assignment, and Miss Applebaum wasn't fair!" Caroline sobbed. "How can I tell Dad and Mom I'm repeating fourth grade? What if we move back to Ohio and I have to tell all my friends, 'Goodbye. I'm going back to fourth grade'?"

"You'll just have to talk to the teacher and ask what you can do for extra credit," said Eddie. "Tell her how sorry you are."

"But what if she wants me to apologize to Wally?"

"That's a tough one," said Eddie.

The girls got to the swinging bridge, but as they started across, they saw that the bridge was already jiggling. The Hatford boys were just walking off the other side, and going right up the hill toward the Malloys' backyard, heading for the garage.

"Oooh, they think they're *so* smart!" Caroline breathed, anger getting the best of her again. "They're just doing this to bother us."

"What do you suppose they want the loft for?" said Beth. "It's not June, after all. It's December. It's *cold* in there."

"There's only one way to find out," said Eddie, smiling slightly.

Beth turned to her sister. "Spy on them?"

"Exactly."

Caroline began to feel all warm inside again, though not, she knew, with the Christmas spirit. Eddie and Beth were back in her corner again, making plans, and that was right where she wanted them to be.

■ ■ ■ ■ ■ ■ ■ ■ ■ ■ ■ ■

# Eight

■

## Peter on the Hot Seat

Jake, Josh, Wally, and Peter trooped into the Bensons' old garage and over to the ladder. It was nailed to the wall and led up through the opening in the floor above.

"Ladder still squeaks," Jake said as he put his foot on the dusty rung and started up, hand over hand.

One by one the boys emerged into the loft. Half the space held window screens and picture frames, and in the other Wally saw an empty box of fireworks, old soda cans, thumbtacks, a mitten, a candy-bar wrapper, string, wire, and a Chinese checkers game. There was not enough room to stand up, but it didn't matter.

"We used to have a lot of fun up here," said Josh.

They looked around some more, crawling over to the loft window, which directly faced the girls' house.

"Remember the time we strung up that pulley between the loft window and Tony Benson's room?" said Jake. "It worked too."

"Yeah, we used to clip notes to the pulley and pass them back and forth."

It was time, however, for the club meeting, and when Jake and Josh and Wally and Peter were sitting in a sort of circle on the floor, Jake said, "Peter, take the hot seat."

Peter, who had been running a little red double-decker Matchbox bus along the floor, quickly looked up. "Why?" he said. And then he saw the sober looks on his brothers' faces. "*What?*" he said.

"Go ahead, take the hot seat," said Wally.

Peter reluctantly crawled into the center of the circle and looked from one brother to the next.

"Okay, how did she get them?" asked Jake, who always seemed to take over.

"I don't *know*!" said Peter, examining the little bus in his hands. "I don't know how Caroline got his clothes."

The boys looked at each other.

"Then how did you even know we were talking about Caroline?" asked Josh.

"How did you know we were talking about *clothes*?" Wally demanded.

Peter was confused. "Well, what *were* you talking about, then?"

"Caroline and my clothes!" said Wally angrily. "You gave them to her, didn't you?"

"Well, she *asked*," said Peter.

"Whose side are you on, anyway?" Wally bellowed.

"If she'd asked you to cut off our heads, would you have done that too?"

"No," Peter whispered.

"What did she pay you, Peter?" asked Josh.

Silence.

"C'mon, what did she give you to steal Wally's clothes?" Josh insisted.

"I didn't steal them, I borrowed them."

"What did she pay you?" Wally yelled.

Wordlessly Peter held out his Matchbox bus.

"A Matchbox car," said Wally disgustedly. "You betrayed one of your brothers for a Matchbox car?"

Peter nodded miserably. "It's a double-decker," he said.

For a while Peter's brothers just sat there staring at him.

"Maybe he's too young to be in our club," said Josh.

Peter's head dropped even lower.

"Either that, or he can't be trusted," said Jake.

Peter's lips began to tremble, and even Wally couldn't stand to see Peter cry.

"Okay, Peter," he said. "You either have to give back that bus or you have to get back every single thing you gave Caroline. I mean *everything*."

"I *will*!" said Peter. "I *told* you she only borrowed them."

There was the sound of voices outside, and the boys suddenly stopped talking and crawled over to peek out the loft window.

"How come they're just getting home from school

now?" Josh whispered. "What have they been doing all this time?"

"Nothing good, you can bet," said Jake.

The four boys watched the girls go in the back door of their house.

"You think they know we're up here?" asked Wally.

"Who cares? Squatters' rights. We've got that official permit from the Bensons, and besides, Mr. Malloy said we could use the loft," said Josh.

Josh took a Magic Marker from his pocket and a sheet of paper from his school notebook. *Explorers' Club: Members Only,* he printed in heavy black letters, and tacked it to the wall.

"Do you really think that will keep Caroline out?" asked Wally.

"Of course not. It will just bug them to death that we're up here," Josh said, grinning.

"I'm hungry," Wally said suddenly. "Let's go home and make a pizza or something."

They climbed down from the loft and Jake said, "All except you, Peter."

"Why?" asked Peter.

"Because you're going to walk out there and knock on the Malloys' door and get Wally's clothes back, that's why," Jake told him. "We'll see you at home."

The three older brothers headed out across the Malloys' backyard and down the hill toward the swinging bridge. Wally turned around once and saw Peter standing forlornly at the Malloys' back door, his head down, knocking with one tightly rolled-up fist.

*Good,* he thought. *Let him be miserable for a while.* Peter had no right to take Wally's clothes and give them to Caroline. Now Wally and Caroline were both in trouble. They'd both failed the December project, and he had no doubt that any day now his folks would receive a letter in the mail from Miss Applebaum, saying, *Dear Mr. and Mrs. Hatford, I very much regret to inform you that your son, Wallace Hatford, is failing the fourth grade* . . .

The water below had an icy look, and the wind whipped at their jackets as the boys moved along the bouncing footbridge. Ducks flew overhead in a V formation as though escorting winter in, and the snow was still coming down.

When they reached the other side, they climbed up the bank and crossed the road.

"What's that?" asked Josh, pointing.

Over on the Hatford steps sat something that looked like a big white ball. A lumpy ball. A ball with a face.

"What *is* it?" Jake wondered aloud, moving closer.

"Underpants!" Wally cried.

"With a face painted on them!" said Josh.

"*My* underpants!" said Wally.

He was right. Caroline had taken all the clothes Peter had given her—all the things she wore when she gave her report—and stuffed them into Wally's underpants until they bulged like a balloon. Then she had painted a smiling face on the seat of the pants.

Wally desperately pulled his baggy blue pants out of the bundle, then his socks and shoes, but he held the underpants up with two fingers. How could he ever put them on again when *Caroline* had been in them? Mom would want to know how the face got on the pants, and if he said "Caroline," she might think Caroline had drawn the picture with him still wearing them.

He'd get even with Caroline, don't think he wouldn't. Wally walked out in the kitchen, where Josh was sticking a pizza in the microwave. There was a note on the table:

**Boys**
**Don't fill up on pizza, we're having steak tonight**
**and I want you to be hungry.**

"We'll be hungry," Josh said to nobody in particular, and waited for the bell to ding. "I want to finish that painting for Mom tonight. Then I've got to think of something for Dad."

"It's you guys I have to shop for," Jake said. "I've already got presents for the folks. Boy, I hope they remember how much I want a skateboard."

As they were eating their second pizza Wally said, "I wonder where Peter is."

"Trying to get your clothes back, when they were here all along," said Jake. "They're probably giving him a hard time. Should we call over there and tell them to send him home? I'll bet he's standing in the hall crying, with Caroline telling him all kinds of lies. Like how she lost Wally's clothes or something, and she's making him look all over their house."

"He'll think twice before he tries that again," said Wally.

The phone rang. It was Mom.

"Everything okay?" she asked.

"Sure. Fine," said Wally.

"You boys didn't eat pizza, did you?"

"It's okay. We're still starving."

"Ask Peter if he turned in his lunch money like he was supposed to."

"Uh . . . I'll ask him when he comes in," said Wally.

"Where is he?"

"Over at the Malloys'."

"The Malloys'? What's he doing there?"

"Uh . . . I'm not sure," said Wally.

"Well, for heaven's sake! Do I have to do everything myself?" Mother said, and hung up.

Wally looked at the others. "What does *that* mean? Maybe we'd better go get him."

"Yeah? Not me," said Jake.

"I don't want to go either," said Josh.

"Listen, you guys. We're all in charge of Peter till Mom gets home, you know. It's not just me," said Wally.

The phone rang again. It was Mom.

"He's baking cookies," she said.

■ ■ ■ ■ ■ ■ ■ ■ ■ ■ ■

# Nine

■

# The Explorers' Club

**B**eth opened the back door to see Peter Hatford standing there, one hand in his pocket.

"What's this? A stickup?" she joked.

Peter didn't understand. He pulled the double-decker Matchbox bus out of his pocket and showed it to her.

"Nice truck," Beth said. "What do you want, Peter?"

"I came for Wally's clothes," he said.

Beth started to laugh. "Wally's *clothes*? Are we running a laundry service now? Hey, Eddie, Peter says he's here for Wally's clothes."

Caroline, who had been pouring herself a glass of orange juice, said, "Come on in, Peter. Tell me what happened."

Peter plunked his bus on the Malloys' kitchen table and sat on the edge of a chair. "Wally was mad."

"Yeah, well, I'm mad too, 'cause we both failed the December project, and maybe the whole fourth grade," she said.

"They said maybe I wasn't old enough to be in their club," Peter said, his lip trembling just a little.

"Ha! *They're* not old enough to be in an Explorers' Club!" said Eddie. "If they're explorers, I'm a fruit fly."

"So, what did they do, Peter? You guys were all up there in the loft. Did they tell you to get Wally's clothes, and then they went on home?" Beth asked.

"Yeah. I'm not supposed to come home without his clothes," said Peter.

"Well, they'll turn up in a little while," Caroline told him.

"Yeah," said Beth. "We were going to bake some more Christmas cookies. Want to help?"

"Chocolate ones?" asked Peter, brightening.

"Chocolate cutouts, peanut butter bars, and short-bread cookies," said Beth.

"Yeah!" said Peter.

"Wash your hands," said Beth, and then to Caroline and Eddie, "This is a riot!"

Caroline rolled out one kind of dough and Beth another. Eddie gave Peter the Christmas-tree cutter and the bell and the Santa, and let him do the cutting. But they had barely got started when the phone rang. It was Mrs. Hatford wondering if Peter was there.

"We're making cookies," Eddie explained.

"Cookies?" Mrs. Hatford asked, surprised. "Is he behaving himself?"

"Oh, yes. He's a big help," Eddie said.

"Well, send him home if he's any bother," Peter's mother told them.

Eddie winked at Caroline. "Now we wait for twenty minutes, and then we call the guys," she whispered.

When the first batch of cookies was out of the oven, Eddie called the Hatfords from the phone in the hallway.

"Hello?" said Jake.

"This is Eddie," Eddie said. "Peter was over here a while ago, and I wondered if I could talk to him again."

There was a pause.

"What time did he leave your place?" Jake asked.

"A long time ago."

Another pause. "Well, he's not here. I'll tell him to call you."

"Thanks," Eddie said, and hung up. She went back to the kitchen and put another pan of cookies in the oven.

About fifteen minutes after that, Beth called the Hatfords.

"Is Peter there?" she asked softly, watching Peter through the doorway. He had a glass of milk in one hand and a cookie in the other.

"No, he hasn't come back yet." It was Wally on the phone this time, and he sounded worried.

"Gee, he should have been there by now. What'd he do? Fall in the river?" Beth asked, teasing. Then she hung up. "Now we've got them hopping," she whispered to Eddie.

When she went back into the kitchen she said, "Well, Peter, it looks as though it's about time for you to go home. You want to take a little bag of cookies with you?"

"Yeah! All chocolate!" he said.

Caroline helped him put on his coat, and he was no sooner outside than the girls heard Wally's voice saying, "Peter, where the heck have you been?"

"I didn't find your clothes, Wally, but I've got some cookies for you," Peter said.

Caroline quickly closed the door, and she and her sisters leaned against the wall, laughing.

*Why am I laughing?* Caroline wondered after a minute. *I can keep teasing Wally Hatford the rest of my life, but I still haven't passed the December project!*

There were car lights on the kitchen wall as Mrs. Malloy drove up from another Christmas shopping trip.

"Mmmm, I smell cookies," she said as she came into the house with two shopping bags.

Caroline had begun to feel more and more lost. Christmas was coming, but it wouldn't seem like Christmas to her, because she was failing fourth grade! Miss Applebaum was probably so disgusted with her that if there was a spring play, Caroline most definitely would not get a part. In fact, Miss Applebaum was probably so disappointed in her that, if the Malloys decided to stay in Buckman, she would tell the fifth- and sixth-grade teachers that when Caroline got to their grades, they should not let her have a part in a play either. Or if they did, she would have to be a tree or a bush or something, certainly not the star.

She was shocked to find that tears were running down her cheeks, and even more dismayed to hear her mother say, "Caroline, what in the world is wrong?"

Instantly she was in her mother's arms, sobbing. But Mrs. Malloy, who had been through more dramas with Caroline than she could count, merely said, "Well, are you going to prison or dying of a fatal disease? Which one is it this time?"

"I'll never make it to college!" Caroline wept.

"Well, dear, then I'll have you around to help me in my old age," her mother said as she let loose of Caroline and began sorting through the things she had bought for their father. "Sit down and tell me about it."

As Beth and Eddie took the last batch of cookies from the oven, Caroline wiped her face on a tea towel and said, "I'll never make it to college, because I'll never get to high school."

"She doesn't think she'll get to high school because she doesn't think she'll get out of elementary," said Eddie.

"And she doesn't think she'll get out of elementary because she won't pass fourth grade," said Beth.

"And I won't pass fourth grade because I've failed the December project!" Caroline said dramatically, flinging her arms wide and bursting into tears again.

"The December project?" asked Mrs. Malloy. "I thought you'd been spending the last two weeks on that report. What happened?"

"She went overboard," said Eddie. "She dressed up in Wally Hatford's clothes."

Mrs. Malloy sat down and listened as the story slowly came out.

"It sounds to me as though it wasn't Wally's clothes that did you in, my dear, but the way you described him to the class. It wasn't flattering, which of course it didn't have to be, but I doubt very much if it was fair."

"But you should have heard what he said about me, Mother! I may be a lot of things, but I am *not* boring!"

"Was that fair?"

"No!"

"Then I guess you're even. Now the two of you have to straighten it out with Miss Applebaum."

*We are not even!* Caroline thought. *We are not even until I give Wally a present for Christmas that will absolutely knock him out. Then, maybe, we'll be even.*

■

The next day Miss Applebaum did not say anything to Caroline or Wally about their reports, nor did either of them bring the matter up. It still seemed much too scary. Caroline and Wally didn't say anything to each other either, and after school, when the three girls were crossing the bridge, Eddie said, "Let's crawl up there and see what they've got in their clubhouse."

"We're not supposed to," said Beth. "Squatters' rights. Dad said they could use the loft."

"They don't *own* it, though. *We're* the ones who are paying the rent on the Bensons' house, remember. I guess if anybody has a right to go up there, we have. We just want to see what the guys are doing."

So they left their book bags on the steps and went

into the garage. Eddie went up the ladder first, then Caroline, then Beth, as Patches, the stray cat, watched sleepily from below.

"Ha!" came Eddie's voice. "*Members Only!* That's a laugh. I now pronounce you a member, Caroline. You too, Beth."

When all three had reached the loft, they knelt in the center of the floor, and looked around.

There were empty soda cans and candy wrappers, a mitten, a newspaper . . . There was also an old tin milk box in one corner, from back in the days when milkmen delivered the milk. It was covered with dust, and Caroline crawled over to look inside.

"Aha!" she cried as she lifted the lid.

"What?" asked Eddie and Beth.

Caroline reached down into the milk box and lifted something out. "Binoculars," she said.

# Ten

■

# Truce

He had his clothes back, but he'd still failed the December project.

Wally sat at the dinner table that night and confessed, while his father stared at him from one end, his mother from the other. Jake and Josh sat across from him, and Peter, who was sitting beside him, stared at his ear.

In the next room, the lights on the Christmas tree twinkled gaily, but it didn't feel like the Christmas season to Wally; it felt like the end of the world.

"How," asked Mr. Hatford, spearing a forkful of lima beans, "can you possibly have written a report so terrible that you failed the whole project?"

Wally swallowed. "I don't know, Dad. I guess I just take stupid pills or something."

"You aren't stupid, Wally. I *know* you knew how to do that assignment. An interview can't be that hard. Something must have made your teacher angry at the way you went about it," his father said.

"She says Caroline and I probably hate each other," Wally told him.

"Why, what a terrible thing to say!" exclaimed Mother. "What would make her think that?"

Jake and Josh rolled their eyes.

" 'Cause they steal each other's clothes," said Peter.

"*What?*" cried Mother and Father together.

"Forget it," said Wally.

"What I want you to do, Wally, is go to school early tomorrow and talk to your teacher. Ask what you can do to earn extra credit and bring up your grade," said his father.

"I'll just spend the rest of my life in fourth, I don't care," said Wally.

"Over my dead body," said his dad.

"He'll just stay in fourth grade long enough for Caroline Malloy to either move back to Ohio or graduate to junior high school; then he'll move on," said Jake, trying not to smile.

"Since when is a son of mine so frightened of a girl that he can't even be in the same grade with her?" asked Mr. Hatford.

It never occurred to Wally that people might think he was *scared* of Caroline. It never entered his head that somebody might think he was chicken.

"I'm not scared of Caroline or anyone," Wally mumbled. "I'll go to school tomorrow and talk to Miss Applebaum."

When he woke the next morning, Wally climbed out of bed before he could change his mind and pulled on his jeans and his sweatshirt with the words I EAT NAILS on the front. Then, after gulping down a glass of juice and half a doughnut, he pulled on his parka, stuffed his hands in his gloves, and tramped down the front steps and off to school. The snow of the day before scarcely measured an inch, and the ground was bare in places.

There were hardly any students on the playground yet. The janitor hadn't even unlocked the front door. Only the teachers' entrance was open.

Wally took a deep breath, walked in the teachers' entrance, and clomped down the hall in his Huskies boots. With his I EAT NAILS sweatshirt showing through the opening of his jacket, he banged through the door of Miss Applebaum's classroom.

There stood Caroline Malloy, talking to the teacher.

"Well, well," said Miss Applebaum. "I seem to have a delegation here this morning. I wonder what's on *your* mind, Wally?"

"I'd like some work for extra credit to make up for the December project," he told her.

"That's very interesting, because this is exactly what Caroline came to say. Since I have no idea why you chose Wally for a partner, Caroline, and then proceeded to stand up here and insult him, or why you, Wally, did your best to insult her, it seems to me that the two of you should decide what you can do to make up the credit. Go sit down at the back of the room and talk to each other while I finish up some work here at my desk."

Wally followed Caroline to the chairs back by the encyclopedias. She sat down on one, and he sat down on another, with one empty chair between them.

Wally half turned toward Caroline, and Caroline half turned toward Wally.

Caroline was staring at her lap. She did not look like the same girl who had stood at the front of the room in Wally's underpants. She didn't look like the same girl who had pretended she had died and been buried in the river, either, or the girl whom Wally and his brothers had locked in the toolshed, the girl who, when they opened the door at last to let her out, had pretended that she had rabies.

This looked like a girl who was afraid she was going to spend the rest of her life in fourth grade and would do whatever it took to pass the December project.

"So what do you want to do?" Wally said at last.

Caroline shook her head. "I don't know. What do you want to do?"

They were quiet for a minute or two.

"I suppose we could ask each other questions all over again and write a better report," said Wally.

"We could if you'll give me better answers," said Caroline.

They agreed.

"So what do you *really* like to eat?" Caroline asked him.

"Pizza, like you said. Chicken McNuggets. Fries," Wally told her.

"And what do you *really* like to do when you're not in school?"

Wally tried not to smile. "When we're not teasing you?" he asked.

Now Caroline was trying not to smile. "Yeah."

Wally put one foot on the rung of the empty chair

between them and thought about it. "I don't know. I just like to . . . fool around, I guess. I mean, I like to float things down the river and see how long it takes them to circle around Island Avenue and reach the other side. I like to explore the old coal mine and camp out at Smuggler's Cove. Things like that. How about you?"

"When we're not trying to bug you guys, you mean?" Now Caroline *was* smiling. "I guess I like to imagine things—how it would feel to be lost in the woods or to be starving to death or to be an old lady—things like that."

Wally started to say, "Isn't that sort of crazy?" but then he remembered that when he'd said he liked to float things down the river, Caroline could have said the same thing about him.

"I suppose we should be writing some of this down," he told her.

"Yeah," said Caroline. They each took out a notebook and began.

On the way home that afternoon, Wally told his brothers about his interview with Caroline and how he was probably going to pass fourth grade after all. And how Caroline had really changed.

"She's not completely crazy," was the way he put it.

"She sure bakes good cookies!" said Peter.

That evening, however, as Peter was watching a Bugs Bunny tape on the VCR, and Mother was busy at the dining room table, which was covered with wrapping paper and presents, Jake looked at Josh.

"Why don't we hold a club meeting?" he said.

"Now?" asked Josh.

"Explorers don't just go out in the daytime," said Jake, and grinned.

"You mean, spy on the girls?" whispered Wally.

"Why not?" said Jake.

Wally thought about it. Why not? The girls knew the guys could be in the loft at any time. If they didn't want to be spied on, all they had to do was pull down their shades.

"Whose room faces the loft?" asked Josh.

"Beth's, I think."

"Okay," said Josh. "Let's do it. But leave Peter behind."

They put on their jackets.

"We've got a little errand to run, Mom," said Jake, poking his head into the dining room, where their mother was putting a label on a box for one of their aunts.

Mom winked. "Okay," she said.

That was the nice thing about Christmas; there were secrets all over the place. If you said you had to go out for a while or you had to run an errand or you were going to your room and didn't want to be bothered, everybody understood. Mom, of course, didn't have a clue, and Dad was still out delivering packages.

Jake carried a flashlight because there was no moon at all. At the bottom of the bank where the swinging bridge began, there was only blackness. They climbed up the bank on the other side and went single file, glad they didn't have Peter to worry about, and made their way to the old garage, around Coach Malloy's car, to the ladder on the side wall. Then they climbed up to the loft.

They crawled across the dusty floor to the window and crowded around it. Wally got the binoculars from the tin milk box and held them to his eyes.

The lights were on in Beth's bedroom. Beth was sitting on the bed talking to Caroline, who was standing in the doorway. The girls seemed to be having an argument.

"Look at the Crazie," said Jake. "She's really teed off about something. Let me see those binoculars for a minute, Wally."

The boys took turns watching through the binoculars. Beth would say something, then Caroline, then Beth, then Caroline. Beth stood up finally, hands on her hips, and leaned forward. Now they appeared to be shouting, though of course the boys couldn't hear what they were saying.

"Boy, I never saw Caroline this mad before," said Wally. "I wonder what it's all about." He didn't even need binoculars to see how angry Caroline was getting.

Through the window they watched Beth shouting back, stamping her foot. She turned her back on Caroline finally, arms folded across her chest.

Suddenly Jake and Josh and Wally gasped in horror, for at that very moment, Caroline picked up a hammer from on top of a dresser, raised it high in the air, and brought it down on her sister's head.

Beth Malloy crumpled to the floor, and the light went out.

# Eleven

■

# A Case of Murder

Eddie had been lying on her bed in the dark in her stocking feet, listening to a new CD, when she happened to look out the window and see a small yellow light bobbing across the swinging bridge and then up the hill toward the Malloys' backyard.

"Beth! Caroline!" she called. "I think we've got company!"

Beth and Caroline had been in Beth's bedroom wrapping a new hammer and pliers and screwdriver set as a Christmas present to their father. They left the paper and ribbon on the floor and hurried into Eddie's darkened room.

"Look out this window," Eddie said. "Down the hill toward the river."

The three girls watched.

"I don't see anything," said Caroline.

"Keep looking," Eddie insisted.

"Looks like the beam of a flashlight," Beth said finally. "I'll bet the boys are back."

"Holding a club meeting at night? In the dark?" said Caroline.

"What do you think? They're spying on us, of course," said Eddie. "And if they're caught, they'll say they're holding a club meeting. Well, *you* know what we do to spies."

"Give them something to talk about!" breathed Caroline excitedly.

"Right!" said Beth.

"I suggest we *really* give them an eyeful this time. I suggest murder," said Beth, who had just finished a book called *The Rise of the Worm People*. "Caroline, why don't you pretend to hit me on the head with a hammer or something. And act like you're really mad! Only be careful to bring the hammer down on the other side of my head, away from the window, so it only looks like it hit me, and I'll crumple to the floor."

"All right!" Caroline said eagerly. "What will you do, Eddie?"

"I'm going to keep out of it. If we're all in the room together, it will look like a put-up job. It will be more convincing if it's just the two of you."

The girls began to giggle.

"They should be going up the ladder to the loft just about now," Beth said. "I'll go in and sit on the edge of my bed, and Caroline, you come in and pretend you're having an argument with me. After a while I'll stomp my foot and turn my back on you, and that's your cue to pick up Dad's hammer and pretend to hit me over the head."

"Got it!" said Caroline. It was wonderful being a team against the boys with Beth and Eddie again.

They could hear Eddie chuckling to herself in the hallway as they took their places.

Caroline, standing in the doorway, moved her arm and shook her fist, her face contorted with anger, but all the while she was reciting the words to "Jingle Bells."

" 'Dashing through the snow, in a one-horse open sleigh,' " she said, glaring at Beth.

" 'O'er the fields we go!' " Beth retorted angrily.

" 'Laughing all the way!' " said Caroline, pleased at how well she and her sister were playing their parts without a trace of a smile.

In the hallway, Eddie was laughing out loud. It was all Caroline could do to keep a straight face.

" 'Bells on bobtail ring, making spirits bright, what fun it is to ride and sing . . .' "

" 'A sleighing song tonight!' " finished Beth, standing up, stomping her foot, and turning her back on Caroline.

Caroline reached over, picked up the new hammer on the dresser, and, holding it up in the air, brought it down in the space between Beth's head and the wall, murmuring, "Now!"

Beth toppled over and collapsed on the floor.

Eddie, waiting in the hall, slipped one hand around the door frame and clicked off the light.

The three girls rolled about on the rug, laughing

hysterically. Finally, when they couldn't laugh anymore, they lay still, grinning up at the ceiling.

"Those guys are so gullible they'll swallow anything," Beth said.

"I'll bet they knew we were fooling, though," said Eddie. "But that's half the fun."

"They'll probably knock on the door and ask Dad if we're all right, just to bug us," said Caroline.

"Wouldn't that be a riot?" said Eddie. "If they do, we'll just turn on the light again and go on wrapping presents and pretend nothing happened. Boys have got to be the dumbest creatures that ever lived."

"Oh, I don't know," said Beth. "Josh isn't so dumb."

"You're always standing up for Josh," Caroline observed.

"Well, he's different from Jake. He's nicer," Beth said.

They stayed on the floor about five minutes in the dark, and had just about decided that nothing was going to happen, that the boys had figured out they were joking, when they suddenly heard a siren coming from downtown Buckman. It seemed to be coming across the road bridge from the business district and heading up Island Avenue. The siren grew louder and louder, and instead of going on past the house, it sounded as though the police car had turned into the driveway. Caroline could see the reflection of the revolving light on the wall of Beth's room.

"Eddie!" she cried in horror, bolting straight up.

Two car doors slammed, one right after the other,

and there were hurried footsteps across the ground, then a loud knock at the front door.

"Dear, can you get that?" the girls heard their mother call.

There was the sound of their father's footsteps crossing the living room, entering the hall, and then the creak of the front door opening.

"Good evening, Coach," came a man's voice. "Is everything all right here?"

"As far as I know," said Mr. Malloy, sounding surprised. "Why? Come on in."

"We got a report about an attack in an upstairs bedroom."

"What?" cried Father.

"Someone was attacked with a hammer. It was an anonymous call."

"Eddie?" came Father's voice from the bottom of the stairs. "Is everything okay up there?"

And before the girls could answer, one of the policemen said, "Do you mind if we look around?"

"Go right ahead," said Father. "Beth? Caroline? The officers are coming up."

The girls were already on their feet, lunging for the light switch. The hammer, the pliers, and the screwdriver were kicked under Beth's bed, and by the time the officers reached the top of the stairs, three girls were seated on the rug in Beth's room, making bows out of Christmas ribbon.

"What's going on?" asked their father, following the policemen into the room.

"What do you mean?" asked Eddie. "We're wrapping presents."

"Did you girls have a fight or anything?" one of the officers asked.

"A fight?" asked Caroline innocently.

"What would we fight about?" asked Beth, putting one arm around Caroline's shoulder, the other around Eddie's.

"Well, we got an anonymous call about an attack up here in one of the bedrooms and thought we ought to check it out," said the policeman.

"I'll bet it was those Hatford boys!" said Eddie. "They're always causing trouble."

"Mind if we check the other rooms to make sure?" an officer asked Dad.

"Please do," said Father. "If there's a body lying around up here, I want to know about it."

The policemen took a quick look in the other rooms, then tipped their caps to Mother, who had come upstairs to see what was going on.

"Sorry to have bothered you folks. Have a good Christmas, now," one of the men said as they went back downstairs.

When the door closed after them, Mother exclaimed, "Now what was *that* all about, do you suppose?"

"I have no idea," said Father. "You know, Jean, maybe it's a good thing we had all girls. If those Hatford boys belonged to us, we'd be in a mental ward."

And upstairs in the bedroom, Eddie, Beth, and Caroline pressed their faces to their knees and rocked with silent laughter.

When all the fuss had died down, however, Eddie

looked mischievously around her. "Call the police on *us,* will they? I think we're entitled to revenge."

The very words made the hair on Caroline's arms stand up in anticipation.

"What are we going to do?" she whispered.

"I'm not sure. I'm thinking," said Eddie. "But maybe, just maybe, the next time they have a meeting of the Explorers' Club—Spy Club, we should call it— we could sneak out there and trap them."

■ ■ ■ ■ ■ ■ ■ ■ ■ ■ ■ ■

# Twelve

■

# Calling 911

"**H**oly smoke!" gasped Jake. "Did you *see* that?"

Even without the binoculars, Josh and Wally saw very well what had happened in Beth's bedroom.

For a moment they stared at each other in horror. Then they went tumbling down the ladder to the floor below and ran like lightning down the hill, across the bridge, and into their house.

Mother was back in the dining room, still wrapping packages, and Dad, who was a sheriff's deputy as well as a postman, had not come home yet.

The boys tore upstairs, where Josh grabbed the phone in the hallway and dialed 911.

"I want to report a murder," he said, breathless, his sides heaving. "Over on Island Avenue . . . the Bensons' house . . . I mean, where the Malloys are now. In an upstairs bedroom." And then he hung up.

From downstairs they could still hear the Bugs Bunny tape Peter was watching on the VCR. Then Mother's footsteps sounded in the hall below.

"Boys?" she called.

"Yeah?" answered Jake, still breathless.

"Are all three of you home?"

"Yeah . . ."

A pause. "Is everything all right?"

"Yeah, we were just having a race," said Wally.

"Okay. If any of you have homework tonight, you'd better get at it," Mother said.

The boys went into the twins' bedroom and shut the door. Then they sat down on the two beds and looked at each other.

"Maybe Caroline didn't kill her. Maybe she only knocked her out," Josh ventured.

"Well, if she didn't kill her, she sure meant to," breathed Wally. They didn't call Caroline the Crazie for nothing, but they hadn't figured she was *that* crazy.

"Think we should have told Coach Malloy instead?" asked Jake after a minute.

"What if he tried to cover up? Say Beth fell and hit her head or something. I mean, wouldn't it be natural?" said Josh.

"Man! I never thought I'd see a real murder!" said Wally. He could still feel his heart racing. "Do you suppose Caroline will confess?"

"No. She'll lie," said Josh. "But if there's a trial, and she does lie, we'll be witnesses."

"You didn't tell the police who you were," Wally reminded him.

"I'm not dumb. I don't want them to think *we* had anything to do with it. Don't tell Mom, either."

"Let's sneak back over and see what happens," said Jake.

They went downstairs again.

"Mom, we forgot something. Be right back," Jake yelled, and they ran across the road, then over the bridge, and up the hill to a clump of bushes some distance from the Malloys' back door.

The policemen were already knocking, and just as the boys reached the bushes, they saw Coach Malloy usher them inside.

"Do you suppose he knows what happened upstairs yet?" asked Josh. "Jeez! Beth! I can't believe it!"

"I'll bet Caroline's made up some lie. She's such a good actress she'll probably get away with it too," said Wally.

"What would make her that mad, though? I've been mad at you guys plenty of times, but I'd never hit you over the head with a hammer," Josh mused.

They could see lights coming on upstairs, then the two policemen moving about from room to room.

"Well, they've found her by now," said Jake. "Any minute they'll call for an ambulance."

"Or a hearse," said Josh.

The boys waited some more.

Much to their surprise, however, when the door opened again, the two officers came out alone. They were not leading Caroline Malloy out in handcuffs. There was no stretcher with a body on it, either. Mr. Malloy and one of the officers were, in fact, shaking hands.

"What?" said Josh, staring.

"Do you suppose Caroline hid the body?" asked Wally.

"Maybe Beth recovered, and was just dazed," said Jake, and the boys watched dumbfounded as the squad car turned around in the clearing and headed back down Island Avenue toward the business district. The back door of the house closed, and the light on the porch went off.

"Wait a minute," said Jake, grabbing his brothers' arms. "The light! Don't you remember? Right after Caroline hit Beth, the light went out."

The three boys looked at each other.

"So who turned it out? Caroline wasn't anywhere near a light switch that I could see, and I had the binoculars," said Jake.

"They *knew* we were watching!" gasped Josh.

"They had it all planned!" croaked Wally. "They must be in there laughing their heads off."

Chagrined, the three boys started back down the hill toward the bridge.

"Listen," said Jake. "We'll say we knew all the time. If they find out we made that call and start teasing us, we'll say the joke's on them. I'll bet Coach Malloy didn't think it was so funny. I'll bet he had plenty to say to Caroline."

"Yeah, we'll get off the first shot. We'll ask *them* whether or not they were grounded for a week."

The boys climbed up the bank from their end of the swinging bridge and started to cross the road. Suddenly, however, Wally grabbed Jake's arm with one hand, Josh's with the other, and pulled them to a stop.

The police car with its red-and-blue lights flashing had circled around in the business district and was coming straight down the road toward them.

Step by step, the boys moved back into the bushes until the squad car passed, but then they watched in shock as it slowed and turned into the Hatfords' driveway.

"Oh, no!" wailed Wally.

"How did they know *we* made the call? I never told them who I was!" said Josh.

"We're dead meat! Roadkill!" moaned Jake. To make things worse, Dad was home.

The two officers got out of the car and walked toward the Hatfords' front porch. When they rapped on the door, it sounded like a hammer pounding in Wally's ears.

It was Mom who answered. In the light from the porch, Wally could see the alarm on her face, and he knew right away she suspected the worst—that he and Jake and Josh had drowned in the river or something.

"Good evening, Ellen," said one of the men. "Don't be alarmed. I just wondered if we could come in for a few minutes."

"Certainly," said Mother. And then Wally heard her call, "Tom? Harry and Joe are here from the police department. I think you'd better come down."

The door closed.

Outside, Wally, Josh, and Jake stared at each other.

"You want to spend the night in the Bensons' garage?" asked Jake.

"How about a one-way ticket to Texas?" moaned Josh.

There had been times in Wally's life when he had thought about running away. Not that he really planned to, or even particularly wanted to. He had just heard now and then about kids actually doing it, and wondered what it would be like—how you knew where to run off to, and what you did after you got there. Now the subject hit him squarely in the face.

The officers didn't stay at the Hatford house very long. It seemed only five minutes, in fact, before the front door was opening again, the men were saying good night to Mom and Dad, and then the squad car backed out of the driveway, without the flashing lights.

Mother went back inside when the police had gone, but Dad did not. Instead he walked to the edge of the porch, cupped his hands over his mouth, and bellowed like a bull moose: "Wallace, Joshua, and Joseph! Get in here! *Now!*"

"You want to spend the night in the woods?" Wally whispered to his brothers.

"He'd just come looking for us," said Josh.

"Heck, we didn't do anything wrong!" said Jake. "Let's go in. All we did was report a crime. What *looked* like a crime, anyway. It's the girls who should be in trouble, not us."

They came out of the bushes as their father yelled again, crossed the road, and went up the steps to the porch, where Mr. Hatford held the door open for

82

them. Whenever Dad held the door open, Wally always felt like a prisoner going into his cell.

"Sit down!" their father thundered.

Peter came in from the other room, eating a Pop-Tart, and watched with wide eyes.

"Okay," said their father. "What happened?"

"What do you mean?" asked Jake and Josh together. Wally decided not to speak unless he had to.

"What was this 'attack' you reported to the police?"

"What attack was that?" asked Josh.

Now Mr. Hatford was getting red in the face. "Don't play dumb with me! Why did you guys call the police and say someone was being murdered upstairs at the Malloys'?"

"Because we saw Caroline hit Beth over the head with a hammer, Dad, and Beth collapsed on the floor, that's why!" said Jake, taking the offensive.

"Wow!" said Peter.

"Didn't Mom always tell us to report a crime? We were just being good citizens," added Josh.

Now Mom was standing in the doorway, her arms folded over her chest. "What, exactly, did you see?"

The boys described the scene in detail, Wally forgetting his vow of silence and filling in whenever a new detail was needed: how Beth was arguing with Caroline, both of them getting angry, Beth stamping her foot and turning her back on her sister, and Caroline picking up the hammer . . .

"We just did like you said, Mom," Josh finished. "We got involved. We reported a crime."

"So you saw it in detail," said Mother.

"Absolutely," said Jake. "As though we were right there in the room."

"Uh-huh," said Mother. "And where exactly *were* you that you could see this so well?"

Wally's heart began to sink.

"They were in the Explorers' Club!" said Peter helpfully. "Looking through the binoculars. You can see really, really good from there."

"What?" said Dad.

"We've got permission from the Bensons to use their loft," Jake bleated. "They signed a paper and everything. We've got squatters' rights to the loft in the garage. We can meet up there whenever we want. Mr. Malloy said it would be okay."

"And the window of this loft faces the girls' bedrooms?" asked Mother.

"Well, just Beth's," said Wally uncomfortably.

"Do you boys mean to tell me that you were sitting up in the Bensons' garage after dark, looking in Beth Malloy's bedroom through a pair of binoculars like some low-down, sneaky Peeping Tom?" Mother cried.

Wally, Josh, and Jake stood like statues.

"We were just holding a club meeting!" Wally squeaked finally.

"A club meeting at nine o'clock in the evening? In twenty-degree weather? You and a pair of binoculars?" said their father. "I'm ashamed of you boys."

Somehow that was the very worst thing Dad could say, Wally decided. That was worse than being whopped on the seat of the pants.

"But—but they know we meet up there!" said Josh. "They know we *could* have been watching. If they didn't want us to see something, they could have pulled down their shades."

"That is disgusting!" said Mother. "I don't want you boys over in that garage again. Do you understand?"

"Don't you think the Buckman police have better things to do than respond to false reports?" asked Dad. "What if there had been a real emergency and they were out wasting their time? This'll be all over the sheriff's office next time I go in."

"Dad, we thought it was real! Honest!" Wally cried.

"Well, either you guys are more gullible than I thought or those girls are terrific actresses," said Dad.

It was really embarrassing. The boys didn't want to admit to either one.

"How did the police know it was us?" asked Wally finally in a small voice.

"The officers called headquarters on their car phone and asked them to trace the call. In case you didn't know, boys, they can trace your call right down to the phone number and the time of day."

"Wow!" said Peter.

# Thirteen

■

# Hot, *Hot* Chocolate

"What we have to do," Eddie told her sisters, "is pretend that absolutely *nothing* happened. The guys are going to be dying to know if we got in trouble, and if they even mention it to us, we don't know what they're talking about. Right?"

"Right," said Caroline.

"And *then*," said Eddie, her eyes beginning to glow, "we wait until they meet in the garage again, and then we trap them."

Caroline had no idea how they were supposed to do that, but she didn't care. They *hadn't* got in trouble, because their parents believed that the Hatford boys were just playing a trick. It was great to have Beth and Eddie back again, thinking of ways to torment the guys, even though Eddie really wanted to make the softball team and Beth was sweet on Josh. The thing about the Hatford boys, they were a ready audience. Boys fell for so many things you wouldn't think they'd believe. It was really incredible. None of her friends back home had been quite so stupid.

Well, *stupid* wasn't exactly the right word, because the Hatfords came up with some pretty good tricks themselves. *Fun* was more like it. And then she put into words something none of them had really said before: "At least the boys are fun."

"And cute," added Beth. "Josh is, anyway. And Peter."

Eddie wrinkled her nose. "Spare me," she said. "I can live without cute. Tell me that Jake or Josh or Wally has anything on his mind besides acting silly, and maybe I'll get interested."

Caroline had never heard her sisters talk like this before.

"Why can't people stay the same, Mother?" she asked later, as they were putting the Christmas bells and holly on the mantel and getting out the holiday candles.

"And whom would we be talking about, I wonder?" said Mother. "Your sisters?"

"Yes. Sometimes they act like they always were, and sometimes they just . . . just act different. Growing weird, is what they are."

"Or maybe just growing up?" Mother suggested.

"Whatever," said Caroline.

When the girls left for school the next morning, West Virginia was having its first big snow of the season. The river had frozen over, and snow was beginning to collect on top of the ice. When the Malloy sisters crossed the swinging bridge, they slid their feet along, rather than risk slipping and falling on the frozen boards. All around them the leafless branches and twigs had taken on a soft furry appearance, and the snow on the roads muted the sound of traffic.

It would have been a perfect morning, Caroline was thinking, if the Hatford boys had not been waiting for them on the other side of the bridge.

"Don't even think it," Eddie said, as she eyed Jake tossing a snowball from one hand to the other.

"Hey, Whomper, Weirdo, and Crazie!" said Jake. "What was all the excitement over at your place last night? We saw a police car pull up. Somebody get murdered or something?"

"They had the wrong address," Beth retorted. "They were looking for *your* place. We sent them back across the river. What was happening at *your* house, anyway?"

Caroline had to admire her sisters. Nobody could think of an answer faster than Beth or Eddie. They'd make good actresses if they wanted to, because they'd be able to cover up when something went wrong. She remembered reading once about a great actress who was onstage during a play with a young, beginning actress, and the phone rang when it wasn't supposed to. As the famous actress lifted the phone and said hello, the young actress was eager to see how she would handle the situation. The great actress handed the phone to her and said, "It's for you."

Caroline thought about that story a lot. If *she* had been the young actress, what would she have said? What would she have done? All she could think of to say was, "Wrong number."

"Nothing happened," said Wally.

"It did so!" said Peter. "Wally and Jake and Josh saw Caroline hit Beth over the head with the hammer!"

"Shut up, Peter!" muttered Wally.

Eddie and Beth burst into laughter as they turned and started up the street toward school. "Boy, you guys sure have big imaginations!" she said.

Caroline was trotting happily between her sisters when suddenly, *Pow! Pow! Pow!*

One snowball hit Beth on the shoulder, another hit Caroline on the leg, and a third landed squarely on the back of Eddie's neck.

Instantly Eddie's book bag was on the ground and her hands were a blur as she packed a snowball. Beth was next, then Caroline, and soon the air was thick with flying snowballs. Peter simply covered his head with his arms and ran on to school while the battle raged.

Eddie didn't just throw, Eddie attacked. She went charging up to Jake and stuffed a snowball right in his mouth. *Pow! Biff! Bam! Poof!*

No telling where the battle would have ended if a teacher hadn't been driving by and honked.

As they picked up their book bags again and headed for school, filling the air with catcalls and hoots, Eddie whispered to Caroline and Beth, "The very next time they come over, we'll be ready."

■

But the next time the boys came over, they were accompanied by their parents, because Mrs. Malloy invited the Hatfords one Sunday afternoon for cookies and hot chocolate—coffee for the adults.

*"Moth-er!"* Eddie had wailed when she found out the Hatfords were coming.

"It's the least we can do after that lovely Thanksgiving dinner they made for us," Mrs. Malloy had said. "Ellen and I checked our calendars, and this was absolutely the only free time we both had. Tom Hatford works such long hours at Christmas."

"But . . . but what will we *talk* about? We can't just sit here staring at each other and stuffing cookies in our mouths!" Beth had protested, and Caroline noticed that her cheeks were strangely pink.

"Why, Beth, we'll talk about whatever comes to mind. With eleven people in a room, it shouldn't be hard to think of something to say. This is our first Christmas in Buckman, and we certainly want to be friendly."

"Our *first* Christmas?" Caroline had asked. "Does this mean there will be a second and a third?"

"We haven't made any decision one way or another, except that we plan to enjoy having the Hatfords over this afternoon," said Coach Malloy.

And so it was that at two minutes to three the doorbell rang, and there were the twins, Jake and Josh, and Wally and Peter, along with their parents. Only the parents and Peter were smiling.

Caroline fully expected Jake and Josh to stuff snowballs down her sisters' necks as they came inside, but as Father welcomed them and took their jackets, she saw that they were empty-handed.

"Welcome!" said the coach, shaking Tom Hatford's hand, then Mrs. Hatford's. "So glad we could find an afternoon to get together."

"Do we get to eat the cookies I helped make?" asked Peter.

"Indeed you do, and more besides," said Mrs. Malloy. "Please come into the living room and sit down, everybody. Boys, do you like marshmallow or whipped cream in your hot chocolate?" She sent Caroline around the room to take orders—regular coffee, decaf, cream, sugar, whipped cream, marshmallow . . .

The parents immediately began talking about the Christmas rush at the post office, interested in Tom Hatford's account of packages that were poorly wrapped and came apart on the conveyor belt. But the Hatford boys seemed interested in making their hot chocolate orders as complicated as possible.

"I'll take whipped cream and marshmallow both, plus a little cinnamon," said Josh, a smile pulling at the corners of his mouth.

"Make that two," said Jake, "but hold the cinnamon and give me chocolate sprinkles instead."

"I want the sprinkles *and* the cinnamon," said Wally.

"I don't want any whipped cream, just marshmallow," said Peter.

Caroline's head swam. *Sprinkles? No sprinkles? Cinnamon? Marshmallow? Who gets what?*

"I'll help," Eddie said quickly, going out into the kitchen with her.

"Me too," said Beth.

As soon as the girls were in the kitchen, Beth and Eddie started to giggle.

*"What?"* asked Caroline.

"Do you know what looks like cinnamon?" said Eddie. "Chili powder."

Caroline gave a little squeak of delight.

"And do you know what looks like chocolate sprinkles?" asked Beth.

"What?" Caroline asked again.

"I don't know," said Beth. "What does?"

The sisters looked through Mother's cupboards. The closest thing they could find to chocolate sprinkles was cracked pepper.

"Now here's the thing—we've got to *mix* them so the guys won't get suspicious. Caroline, you mix a little cinnamon and chili powder together, Beth, you do the chocolate sprinkles and cracked pepper, and I'll get the coffee for Mr. and Mrs. Hatford."

"Ha! Wally wanted both the chocolate and cinnamon. He's going to get a double dose!" laughed Caroline. Was this a good party or what?

At last the tray was ready. Beth carried it in, followed by Eddie with the coffee. Mother and Dad were sitting with the Hatfords around the coffee table, which had been covered with a holiday tablecloth that reached to the floor, embroidered with poinsettias and holly.

"One plain with marshmallow," Caroline said politely, handing the first cup to Peter.

She picked up the next one. "One whipped cream and marshmallow with cinnamon," she said, and handed it to Josh. "One whipped cream and marshmallow with chocolate sprinkles." She handed that one to Jake.

Then she turned to Wally: "And one cup with everything."

Eddie carefully poured the coffee and the decaf into the appropriate cups and passed them to the grownups, setting the sugar and the creamer on the coffee table beside the huge platter of Christmas cookies of every design—round and square, frosted and plain, decorated and drizzled—roll-ups, sandwich style, bars, drop cookies, and cutouts.

Then she and Beth and Caroline sat down demurely on the big sofa across from the four boys, while the parents seemed to prefer the armchairs.

"Ummm! This is good! It's the best hot chocolate I ever tasted," said Peter, wiping his mouth on his sleeve and reaching for the largest Santa cookie on the platter.

Mrs. Malloy smiled. "I was hoping you'd take that one, Peter. I made it especially for you."

"You did?" Peter said.

But his words were drowned out by sudden coughing from Wally, whose face was quickly turning red. Wally's eyes watered.

"Gracious!" said his mother.

Jake was next; he sneezed.

"I certainly hope it's not the cocoa," said Mrs. Malloy, looking puzzled.

"Oh, no," said Jake, patting his chest. "It's delicious. Just went down the wrong way, I guess."

Josh took a drink of his, and blinked as his eyes too began to smart. "Good cocoa," he said.

Caroline, Beth, and Eddie stared. They were actually going to drink it! The boys were really going to sit there and pretend they didn't notice a thing. Caroline couldn't help admiring Wally. She doubted *she* could have pretended it was okay, and *she* was supposed to be an actress!

The grown-ups went on talking about all sorts of boring things.

"So there you have it!" Mrs. Hatford was saying. "The county and the college both want the three acres, and I suppose the voters will have to decide . . ."

Caroline watched as Wally took another small sip of hot chocolate and fought off another coughing fit.

Suddenly her eyes went from Wally to the big ceramic platter of cookies, for as Jake reached for another cookie, the platter suddenly jiggled up and down. Jake pulled back his hand and stared. Then he reached out once more, and again the platter began bouncing.

"Josh . . . ," he said, and nudged his brother.

Caroline was already nudging Beth and Eddie.

"The cookies!" she whispered.

Peter was over by the window, running his new Matchbox double-decker along the sill, leaving his three brothers and the three Malloy sisters staring silently at the cookie platter.

"What?" murmured Beth when Caroline poked her.

"The . . . the cookies! They moved!" Caroline whispered back.

They all focused on the platter. Nothing happened.

"You're out of your mind," said Eddie.

"No, they did!" Caroline insisted.

"I saw them too," said Jake. "You take one, Josh."

Josh put out his hand and just as he did so, the platter began dancing again.

Josh quickly withdrew his hand.

"It's some kind of trick the girls are pulling on us," he said.

"No, honestly!" said Beth, who had seen it now. "I don't know what's causing that."

"Well, take one anyway!" said Wally, and he reached for a pinwheel cookie in the middle of the assortment. This time the platter leaped so violently that two of the cookies on one end slid off.

Wally dropped the pinwheel and gaped.

"Boys?" said Mrs. Hatford.

Wally turned sheepishly. "It's . . . the platter. It keeps moving."

"It what?" asked his father.

"See?" said Wally. He stretched out his hand for another cookie. Nothing happened.

Josh reached for a cookie. Then Jake. Nothing happened.

Peter came over to look, and as soon as he put out his hand, the platter again leaped and danced.

"Yipes!" cried Peter, and backed away.

"Now, George, what are you up to?" Mrs. Malloy laughed, and at that, Coach Malloy revealed a narrow green rubber tube stretching from the palm of his hand down the side of his chair, under the throw rug, up under the cloth on the coffee table, to a spot right beneath the cookie platter. Whenever he pressed on the rubber bulb in the palm of his hand, it sent air through the tube into a little pouch at the other end, which made the platter jump.

"Heck, with all the pranks our kids have been playing lately, I decided they shouldn't have all the fun!" Mr. Malloy said, and the other grown-ups laughed with him.

"Absolutely not," said Mr. Hatford. "Why, I remember that trick when I was young. We used to get the turkey rising and falling on Thanksgiving."

Everyone laughed then, and of course each of the Hatford boys had to try it. When the party ended at four-thirty and the Hatfords prepared to leave, Wally was in the hallway in his jacket, ready to go, when he looked up to see that he was standing under a sprig of mistletoe. He shot out of the house like a cannonball, and Caroline, Eddie, and Beth were still laughing when they cleared the coffee table later and took the cups to the kitchen.

■ ■ ■ ■ ■ ■ ■ ■ ■ ■ ■

# Fourteen

■

# Letter to Georgia

Dear Bill and Danny, Steve, Tony, and Doug:

Thought you'd like to know that the police were over at your house the other night. Caroline Malloy, the Crazie, went after her sister with a hammer. Missed, but I can imagine what the hammer did to the floor. They are really weirdos.

I'm going to pass fourth grade by the skin of my teeth. Crazy Caroline chose me for her partner for Miss Applebaum's December project. We had to interview each other. Then we had to pretend we were each other for a day, and write a report to read aloud in front of the class. I'll bet your Georgia-peach teacher doesn't come up with anything that dumb, Danny.

What I'd like about now is to change places with one of you guys and be you for a day. I'd gladly go down there for a week if one of you wants to come here and see what life with the Malloys is really like.

See what you got us into by moving down to Georgia?

Wally (and Jake and Josh and Peter)

■ ■ ■ ■ ■ ■ ■ ■ ■ ■ ■

# Fifteen

■

# Trapped

The Malloy sisters were surprised to see the Hatfords heading for the garage again on Monday, going across the swinging bridge just ahead of them. They had supposed that after the fiasco with the police, Mr. and Mrs. Hatford might have forbidden them to go up in the loft again, and knew they were right when Peter, tagging along behind his brothers, looked back over his shoulder and called, "We're not supposed to go up in the loft again, but we came back to get our binoculars."

"Peter! Shut up!" they heard Jake mutter.

There was a certain swagger to their walk that irritated Eddie, it seemed. A certain grin on their faces that made Caroline herself frown. The girls could only watch as the boys loped across the clearing as though they owned the place and marched right into the garage. It didn't take four boys to retrieve a pair of binoculars.

"Okay, that's it! Plan B!" said Eddie.

As luck would have it, Mother was at a meeting of the faculty wives. There was a note on the table saying she'd be home about six, and they could heat up a pan of chili if they wanted dinner early.

"Perfect!" said Eddie. "Absolutely perfect!"

She told Beth and Caroline that for several days she had been working out the details of what they were going to do the next time the boys came over, and promptly explained her plan.

Knowing that the Hatfords would be looking out of the loft window facing the house, Caroline and Beth, in their winter jackets and mittens, came out the back door with a shovel. With much whispering, they began to dig a hole in the snow around the corner of the house, just close enough that the boys could still see them.

From the quiet in the garage, they knew very well that the boys were watching. They had to put on a convincing show, because the point was to keep the boys glued to the loft window long enough for Eddie to sneak out the front door of the house, and around the bushes where the boys couldn't see, and enter the garage from another door. And then, while the Hatfords on the floor above were watching the girls outside, wondering what Beth and Caroline were up to, Eddie, armed with a can of brown paint and a brush she had found in the Bensons' basement, would secretly, silently, paint the rungs of the ladder.

"What the heck are they *doing*?" Caroline heard Jake mutter from up in the loft. There was the squeak of floorboards as the boys scooted around, changing places to see out the small window. The frozen earth beneath the snow was hard, and difficult to dig, but the girls kept chopping away.

"Why don't we act as though we're burying something?" Beth whispered finally. "What do you bet they'll come back here some night and try to dig it up?"

Caroline tried not to laugh. "Okay. Pretend it's in my pocket, and you take it out."

Caroline straightened up, holding the shovel out in front of her while Beth reached over and thrust one hand into her jacket pocket. Then, making a tight fist, she lowered her arm into the hole in the snow and stood up again. More whispering.

"How long are we supposed to stay out here?" Caroline asked.

"Till Eddie gets back inside and comes to the door to get us. Then we'll know she's done."

The two girls got down on their hands and knees and peered down into the hole. Then they began putting the earth back, then the snow, packing it down and taking their time about it.

"What do we do now?" whispered Caroline.

"I don't know. Dig another hole? We have to keep their attention until—"

At that moment the back door opened and Eddie called, "I'm making popcorn. Anybody want some?"

"I do!" came Peter's voice from the loft.

"Peter, shut *up*!" Josh told him.

"So you guys are still up there?" Eddie yelled. "Don't you think it's time you went home?"

"We'll go when we're good and ready," Jake replied.

"Fine. What do we care?" said Eddie, as her sisters trooped inside. They shut the door behind them. "Now," she said laughing, "it's only a matter of time till they discover they're trapped. Might as well go make the popcorn. Then we can take it outside, sit in the garage, and watch the show."

It took only a few minutes in the microwave to pop a bag of corn, and the girls poured it into a metal bowl and went back out to the garage, grinning. They sat cross-legged in their jackets on the dirt floor, facing the ladder, and waited.

"This is more fun than a movie," said Beth.

From time to time there came voices from up in the loft, the sounds of the boys horsing around, and finally one booted foot appeared through the small opening in the floor above, then another.

"Wally, I'll bet," whispered Caroline, stuffing another handful of popcorn into her mouth.

Suddenly the air was filled with yelps and cries.

Wally had come down only two rungs and Jake's foot had just appeared, when Wally began yelling, "Jake! They've painted the ladder! I've got paint on my hands!"

"Oh, no!" yelled Jake. "I've got it on the leg of my jeans!"

"I can smell it!" called Josh.

Wally leaped to the floor below, Jake wavered a moment, still holding on with one hand; then he too dropped the eight feet to the floor.

The girls stopped eating. Somehow that was not the way they had imagined it. They had thought the boys would discover that the ladder was painted *before* they started down, and would stay in the loft. Now there were two boys up and two boys down.

"We're trapped up here!" yelled Josh.

And Peter's sorrowful cry: "You mean we have to spend the night here and can't have any food?"

Jake wheeled about and saw the girls.

"You're in big trouble! I've got paint on my new jeans!" he said.

"What do you mean, *we're* in trouble?" said Eddie. "You know you weren't supposed to come back up here again."

"We only came to get the binoculars! You can't hold us prisoner!" yelled Peter from the floor above.

Eddie laughed. "Joke: How many Hatfords does it take to retrieve a pair of binoculars? Four: one to get the binoculars, two to get paint on their clothes, and one to do the yelling."

"Go outside and stand under the window, Jake!" Josh called down.

Jake and Wally went outside, and the girls followed, still eating their popcorn. Josh was dangling Peter from the high open window. There wasn't any glass at all.

"Catch!" Josh yelled. "One, two, three . . ." And down Peter came, into the arms of Jake and Wally.

Caroline stopped eating. She hadn't dreamed that the boys would actually come out the loft window, and she could tell by the look on Eddie's face that Eddie hadn't either. What if somebody got hurt? Broke an ankle or something?

Now Josh was preparing to jump. One of his feet

appeared out the loft window, then his whole leg, then a second leg.

"Boy, I hope they leave before Mom gets here, or we'll get it!" Eddie whispered. "Come on, Josh! Jump!" she said loudly.

Beth covered her eyes.

"Maybe we should drag out a mattress or something," Caroline suggested.

But it was too late for that.

"One, two, three . . . jump!" Jake instructed.

Josh was dangling by his hands now to shorten the drop, and he let go. A second later he fell in a heap on top of Wally and Jake.

Eddie gave a sigh of relief when all four boys were finally on their feet and were slinking off toward the bridge, casting glowering looks at the girls over their shoulders.

"We're lucky we got out of *that* one!" said Beth. "You don't suppose their mom will call our mom about the paint on their clothes, do you?"

"They'd have to admit they were back in the garage again if they told," said Eddie. "My guess is that they'll keep all this very, very quiet."

They went back inside, cleaned up the kitchen, and were diligently doing their homework on the dining room table when they heard Mother's car come up the drive and park outside the kitchen window.

"Your father's still at the college," she said when she came in. "Some big reception for alumni or something. How are things going here?"

"Nothing special," said Beth. "We're all doing homework."

Mother went upstairs to change her clothes, and the girls cast each other relieved glances and bent over their books again. Caroline was finishing the last of her report on Wally Hatford, and was finding only good things to say about him. Miss Applebaum would be impressed. It was easy saying nice things about a person when you had just won a major battle.

Mother came downstairs in green sweatpants and shirt and turned on the lights on the Christmas tree. Then she put a CD of carols on the player and set about making dinner, just as the headlights of Father's car swept across the kitchen walls.

"Dinner in ten minutes, girls," she called. "I think we'll just eat in the kitchen tonight. Chili and crackers, that's it."

There was the sound of Father's car idling in the garage, then the engine went off. A door slammed. And finally he came through the back door.

"Jean?" he called. "What am I smelling? Are you painting something?"

Mother came out of the pantry. "Painting? Of course not."

"Well, there's a strong paint smell coming from somewhere."

"Really?" said Mother. She walked over and stuck her head out the back, then closed the door behind him. "Why, George!" she said suddenly. "You've got fresh paint on your good jacket! That's where the smell is coming from. There are stripes all across the back of your sport coat. It's ruined! Where in the world have you been?"

# Sixteen

■

# Another Letter to Georgia

*Dear Bill and Danny, Steve, Tony, and Doug:*

*We thought you might like to know that the Whomper painted your garage.*

*We've been meeting up in your loft and they got smart and thought they could trap us up there. When we came down I got paint on the sleeves of my jacket and Jake got some on his jeans. Josh and Peter had to jump.*

*It took us about an hour to get the paint out with turpentine, and we didn't dare tell Mom what happened because we weren't supposed to go back up there again. Boy, I'll say one thing for those Malloys: There isn't a dull moment with them around. Jake is really teed off at them, but if you want the truth, I think Josh sort of likes Beth a little.*

*If they decide to stay in Buckman after you guys come back, we sure could have a lot of fun teasing them. Can you imagine how turned around we could get them if we ever took them to the old coal tunnel in the hill? And what about that field that gets so muddy in the spring? Caroline's so short she'd probably sink in up to her armpits.*

*Right now, though, we've got snow. I'll bet you haven't seen any of that down in Georgia. Had a snowball fight the other morning with the girls, and Eddie went a little bonkers. You don't exactly want to mess with Eddie.*

*As usual, Buckman looks great at Christmas. There are wreaths up downtown and everything. Three of my uncles are coming for Christmas. They come every year, remember? We have to give up our bedrooms and sleep in sleeping bags in the living room, but that's okay.*

*Danny, you going to give your Georgia-peach teacher a present for Christmas? I'm not giving Miss Applebaum anything.*

*Merry Christmas, you guys.*

*Wally (and Jake and Josh and Peter)*

# Seventeen

■

## Slave Labor

Coach Malloy stood in the living room, facing his wife and three daughters, a new sport coat on his arm.

"Well," he said, "the dry cleaner says it can't be cleaned. He can get some of the paint out but not all, and there's no way I can wear it to meetings again. So I've bought a new one, and here, girls, is the bill." He walked over and handed it to Eddie.

Eddie gulped. Since she had done the actual painting and it had been her idea, it was she who would be most severely punished. Their father's decision was this: Since all three girls had knowingly participated in the prank, all three were responsible for earning the money it would cost to pay for a new sport jacket.

"Dad, I don't mind working to pay for it, but this is a lot of money! I could still be looking for jobs to do when it's time to try out for the softball team!" she said.

"That, I'm afraid, is your problem," he told her.

"Lock me up with bread and water, but *please* don't keep me off the team!" Eddie pleaded.

"That's entirely up to you," Father said. "You'll just have to work doubly hard between now and try-outs, won't you?"

Caroline swallowed. She knew that, ever since they had moved to West Virginia, her sister had dreamed about trying out for the Buckman Elementary softball team, sure that she could outhit and outpitch every boy in town. This past fall Beth and Caroline had helped her practice in a field behind the college, and Caroline imagined she could still hear the crack of the bat against a ball as Eddie hit a homer; she could see her sister's muscles tighten as she wound up for the pitch. And now . . .

Eddie passed the bill for the sport coat to Caroline and Beth.

"We could buy you a new car for this!" squeaked Caroline in dismay.

"Hardly," said her father. And then he added, "Eddie, I want you to call the Hatford boys and apologize. Ask if any of their clothes were ruined, and if they were, you can add those to your bill."

"Dad!" Eddie choked. "They weren't supposed to be up there in the first place."

"That's between them and their parents, and that's not the point. You had no business doing any painting in the garage and you know it—a garage we don't even own." Then he went upstairs to hang up his new jacket.

Caroline stared at her sisters. Calling the boys to apologize was the worst punishment of all.

"I'll do it," Beth said grimly. "We're all in this together. I'll ask to speak to Josh. If anyone will understand, it's him."

They waited until their father came downstairs; then they went up, took the phone from their parents' bedroom, and dragged it into Beth's.

Beth sat down on the floor, set the phone in her lap, and took a deep breath. She dialed the Hatfords' number. Eddie and Caroline sat on the floor across from her.

"Hello," said Beth. "Is this Peter? Could I speak to Josh, please?"

There was a pause.

"No," Beth said. "I'm not going to say something mean to him. Just put him on, will you?"

Caroline rested her head on her knees and closed her eyes.

"Josh? Hi, this is Beth. Listen, I just wanted to say that we're really sorry you guys got paint on your clothes. Wally and Jake, I mean. I guess the joke got a little out of hand."

Eddie stared at her. *"Sorry?"* she mouthed.

Another pause.

"Well, Dad wanted me to call over and see if any of their clothes were ruined. He got paint on his jacket, and he's really mad, and he said if we ruined any of your stuff we have to pay for that too."

This time Eddie put her face on *her* knees. Caroline was beginning to be worried. She hadn't thought Beth would apologize quite that much. Why, the guys could say *all* their clothes were ruined, and make the Malloy sisters their slaves for the rest of their natural lives!

But then she heard Beth say, "Really? Are you sure? Well, I had to find out. Thanks a lot, Josh. I really appreciate it." And Beth hung up.

"What's all this 'sorry' business?" Eddie demanded. "And why did you have to tell them about Dad's jacket?"

"Everything's okay," said Beth. "They got the paint out themselves with turpentine, and we don't owe them anything."

Now Caroline and Eddie stared.

"Really?" said Eddie. "Nothing?"

"Not a cent."

"I don't believe it!" said Eddie.

"Well, *sometimes* it pays to be nice," Beth told her.

"Whew!" said Caroline, leaning back against the wall. "Now all we have to do is figure out how to earn a hundred and seventy-five dollars to pay for Dad's jacket."

"I can bake," said Beth. "I could take orders every week for banana-bread muffins and bake them on Saturdays. Peanut butter cookies, too. Maybe I could offer to make Christmas cookies for people too busy to bake."

Caroline tried to think what she could do. The thing she was best at, of course, was acting, but she doubted that anyone would want to pay her to come into their living rooms and do a dramatic reading.

"Maybe I could perform for little kids' birthday parties," she said. "Read them stories and stuff."

Eddie herself preferred the more physical jobs. She wanted to keep her body lean and limber. If it had been spring, she could have offered to wash windows or paint walls or clean up yards, but nobody had that in mind in December.

"I'll do housecleaning," she decided. "There must be busy people who are getting ready for the holidays and would like someone else to do the scrubbing."

It was probably their greatest humiliation that the Malloy girls had to go around two Saturdays before Christmas, putting signs on telephone poles, in shop windows, on trees—wherever they were allowed to post one—offering their services. They could see the Hatford boys watching them from a distance, hiding an amused grin behind their hands or disguising a chuckle with a cough. Even Josh seemed to think it was funny.

Eddie got a number of calls about housecleaning and was encouraged. With company coming, people told her, and all there was to do at Christmas, they were glad to pay to have their houses cleaned.

Beth also got a few orders for Christmas cookies, so she worked every afternoon when she got home, making chocolate Rice Krispies creations, fudge bars, almond rounds, and lemon squares. There was hardly time to do her own Christmas shopping and wrapping, and the lavender scarf she'd been knitting for Mother still sat in her yarn basket.

Caroline was the most disappointed.

"Doesn't anyone want to hire a budding young

actress to perform at birthday parties?" she asked her family in desperation. "Isn't anyone even *having* birthdays around Christmas?"

She got only one request to entertain three small children one afternoon while the mother did her Christmas wrapping, but the oldest had a cold and needed Caroline to blow his nose every five minutes, the second child cried the whole time, and the youngest fell into the toilet. Nobody wanted her to sing or recite a scene from *The Wind in the Willows,* and Caroline was even more glad than they were when their mother had finished her chore.

If Beth had any bad feelings left toward the Hatford boys, she didn't talk about them.

If Eddie wished she were back in Ohio, she never said.

Perhaps because Caroline had the least to do, it was she who resented the fact that she and her sisters had to work so hard to pay for Dad's jacket. She knew they were responsible, of course, but if the boys had stayed across the river where they belonged, nothing would have happened.

Never mind that she was the one who had seemed to like Buckman the most. Never mind that she loved thinking up new ways to annoy Jake and Josh and Wally, and sometimes even Peter. The fact was that everybody else was busy, and she was not.

And so, with the angel wrapping paper and the blue crinkle ribbon that Mother had bought at the hardware store, Caroline wrapped, in a small flat box, the grossest thing she could find to give to Wally Hatford, and set it by the pile of presents waiting to be delivered there by the door. Inside was a little puddle of cat vomit that Patches, the stray cat, had deposited on the Malloys' back steps. There was a big fat hairball in the middle of the vomit and, if you looked closely, you could even find a piece or two of undigested mouse feet.

■ ■ ■ ■ ■ ■ ■ ■ ■ ■ ■ ■ ■

# Eighteen

■

# Mistake #1

The week before Christmas was always the busiest time in the Hatford household.

Mr. Hatford was late getting home every night. Each year, it seemed, people mailed their Christmas cards and packages later and later, and the boys' father might be out till six or seven o'clock trying to get everything delivered by Christmas Eve.

"Just don't do it, Tom!" Wally's mother would say. "If people don't think enough of their aunt Emma to buy her a present in time, then I don't see why you need to knock yourself out trying to deliver it by Christmas Eve."

But then she would remember a present *she* had forgotten to buy for somebody, and so—each year was the same, with Mrs. Hatford and the boys doing the wrapping and decorating by themselves.

The boys didn't talk about the Malloys much. For one thing, they hardly even saw Eddie, Beth, and Caroline, the girls were so busy trying to earn money to pay for the jacket. In the days that followed, however, with the girls' signs on trees and light poles all over Buckman, advertising their jobs, Josh said he was feeling a little bit sorry for them. And with Christmas only a few days off, Wally, perhaps, should have been thinking about forgiveness too. But he couldn't quite forgive them yet, because there was one little joke he had up his sleeve that was too good to pass up.

He had to admit he was a little bit mad—no, a *lot* mad—that he had got paint on the sleeves of his jacket. But he was also still mad at Caroline for wearing his clothes to school. He could forgive her for wearing his trousers, maybe, and his T-shirt, his socks and shoes, but his *underpants*? Was there any boy in Buckman who would like to have his underpants displayed in public by a girl who was *wearing* them?

Most boys, he figured, would have decontaminated them. Most boys, in fact, would probably have thrown them out. Wally himself was certainly never going to wear them again, especially underpants that had a happy face painted on the seat, but he had big plans for those underpants.

A few days before Christmas, he put them in a box and wrapped them in the angel-print paper that Mother had brought home from the hardware store. It was the blue-and-gold paper that the hardware store was selling at half price. He put the box aside to take to school on the last day before the Christmas holidays, to put in Caroline's book bag.

He was afraid she might guess who it was from, and if she did, she'd probably throw it in the Buckman

River without opening it. So he didn't even put her name on it, just a little folded piece of paper under the ribbon that read, "From a secret admirer," so she'd be *sure* to open it. He no more admired Caroline than he admired stinkweed. When she saw the underpants, though, with another note—"Since you liked them so much, you can have them"—she'd know Wally was no admirer.

The day before vacation, Wally ate his breakfast as usual, and when no one was looking, he went into the living room to get the little box off the mantel. At least he *thought* he had put it on the mantel. He wanted it someplace he would see it every day so he would not forget it, but now he didn't know where it was. There were small flat boxes and rectangular boxes, but not the square box he had used to hold the underpants.

"Mom!" he yelled. "Where's that box I wrapped the other day? I have to take it to school."

"There are boxes all over this house, Wally. Which one do you mean?" she called back.

"The square one in the angel wrapping paper. I left it on the mantel, I think."

"There were four boxes on the mantel, and they all had the angel wrapping paper," his mother answered. "I have no idea which one you're talking about."

Wally's heart began to pound. This was too good a joke to get lost somewhere.

"Well, it's not here, and I've got to find it," he said.

"Who was it for?" his mother asked, coming to the doorway.

Wally felt he could not possibly tell her it was for

Caroline. He knew she would demand to know what was in it. Mom could smell trouble a mile away.

"For my teacher," he fibbed.

"Well, how nice! You'll have to find it without my help, though, because I've got a ton of things to do before I leave for work this morning," she said.

Wally kicked snow all the way to school that morning. He couldn't believe his great joke was ruined. All that work to wrap up the package like it was something really special, and now it was gone. Whoever got it wouldn't even understand the joke, and if Wally found it later, it would be too late to take it to school and slip it into Caroline's book bag.

"Hi, Wally," Caroline said when he walked into the classroom. She didn't poke him in the back with her ruler, either. "Merry Christmas." And to Wally's surprise, he found a present sliding over his shoulder, falling into his lap. Was this her way of apologizing for the paint prank, maybe?

Fortunately, no one seemed to be looking, but Wally felt his ears burn anyway—partly at getting a gift from a girl, partly because the girl was Caroline, and partly because he knew what he had *almost* given her.

"Uh . . . thanks," he said, and stuffed it into his desk before anyone could see it. If Caroline thought he was going to open it here in the classroom in front of everyone, she was crazy.

He felt uncomfortable all morning with Caroline sitting behind him on her best behavior. Was it possible that after all the stuff they had done to make each other miserable, she liked him anyway?

Wally bolted through the door at recess, keeping as far away from Caroline as possible, and sat on the other side of the lunchroom from her at noon. He was never so glad as when school was over for the day. He crammed Caroline's present to him into his book bag, then set out for home with his brothers, glad that the Malloy girls were already far ahead.

The boys were almost a block from home when they heard the light tap of a horn behind them and turned to see Mother's car pulling over toward the curb.

Mrs. Hatford rolled down her window.

"I took the afternoon off to do some Christmas errands," she told them. "I should be home in about an hour. Wally, I found that gift you wrapped and just dropped it off at the school. I told Miss Apple-baum you couldn't find it this morning but wanted her to have it."

Wally's jaw dropped to his chest. *"What?"* he said.

"That box you wrapped. You left it on the book-case. I just gave it to your teacher, so you don't have to worry about it anymore."

Mother drove away, and Wally wondered if you could have a heart attack when you were only nine years old. Without a word to his brothers, he whirled about and ran as fast as he could back to the school, his book bag banging against him. His teacher had just received a gift that said, "From a secret admirer," and a note with his underpants saying, "Since you liked them so much, you can have them." He would probably be thrown out of elementary school and sent to a military academy.

He had to stop this. His sides began to ache, his forehead to sweat. He tore up the driveway to the school and around to the faculty entrance. Then he stopped, because Miss Applebaum's car was just pulling out of the parking lot, and then went rolling down the street.

■

*Dear Wally (and Jake and Josh and Peter):*

*Man, the Malloy girls must be something! Painting our garage?*

*I wonder if there will be anything left of our house to come back to—if we come back, that is.*

*Dad's been offered a job here in Atlanta for next year, but he doesn't know yet if he's going to take it. There are a lot of things we'll miss up there in Buckman if he does. Christmas is going to be really weird down here with the weather so warm. We'll miss the snow most of all.*

*We've got a present for Danny's teacher, though—the one who's a Georgia peach. Man, she's pretty. We're thinking of giving her one of Mom's special batches of brownies, maybe. Why don't you give Miss Applebaum a jar of dill pickles?*

*Merry Christmas! Make sure the Malloys' tree doesn't catch on fire and burn down our house!*

*Bill (and Danny, Steve, Tony, and Doug)*

■ ■ ■ ■ ■ ■ ■ ■ ■ ■ ■

# Nineteen

■

# Mistake #2

Coach Malloy did not care for Christmas shopping. Each year, instead of a present, he gave his wife a catalog and asked her to choose from it whatever she liked. He left shopping for the girls to his wife as well. This year, in fact, Mother had to choose a gift for his secretary, and also for the receptionist who answered the phone for the whole department.

"I'm about shopped out," Mother said as the family enjoyed a late breakfast. "Two days till Christmas." And then, turning to her husband, "Is there anyone else at the college we've forgotten who might be expecting a present from you?"

"I don't think so," Coach Malloy said, looking for the sports section, finding it, and dropping the rest of the newspaper onto the floor. "What did you buy the women in my office?"

"I ordered a box of pears for the woman who answers the phone, but I thought your secretary deserved something more personal. You said she was engaged to be married, didn't you?"

"Yes."

"Well, I found a small carved wooden box to keep notes and love letters in. I think she might appreciate that."

"Sounds good to me," said Mr. Malloy.

Caroline was glad she did not have to shop for presents for secretaries. It was all she could do to buy gifts for her family. Her biggest inspiration of all, however, was Wally Hatford's present—the cat vomit with the hair ball and the piece of undigested mouse in it. She was dying to know if he had opened it in the rest room at school, or at home, or was saving it till Christmas morning.

Everyone seemed to be relaxing and enjoying the weekend. Eddie had only one more house to clean, the morning before Christmas. Beth, however, had an order for six dozen cookies to be delivered by Christmas Eve, and the woman wanted them fresh. Beth had to get up early the next morning to bake all day. It was not how she had hoped to spend Christmas Eve day, but it had to be done.

Mrs. Malloy had gone out to empty the garbage after breakfast when she called, on her way back inside, "Package for you, Caroline. I didn't think Mr. Hatford had been here already. It was just sitting on the back steps. Now why would he put it there?"

Caroline took one look at the box and figured Wally had given *her* a present in return—something even grosser than cat vomit. She took it to her room, then had second thoughts and took it out to the garage instead. Maybe she should call the bomb squad to open it. It was probably something that would explode in her face.

It was wrapped in the same angel-print paper that she had used to wrap her gift to Wally. In fact, it looked like the very same present she had slipped over his shoulder. Caroline stood in the middle of the floor and, holding one corner of the wrapping paper, shook it loose from its contents.

Out tumbled a small wooden box, engraved with hearts and flowers. The word *Letters* was carved on the lid, which could only mean love letters, surrounded as it was with cupids and stuff.

Caroline gasped. The secretary's present! For the woman who was about to be married! Somehow she had picked up the wrong present and given Wally Hatford a box for love letters! This was a terrible mix-up! In horror, she opened the lid, and there was a note in Wally's handwriting: *Yuuuck! Wally Hatford.*

Then who . . . ?

Caroline felt weak in the knees. She tore into the house and looked up Dad's secretary's name in the phone book. Then, afraid to ride her bike on the icy streets, she stuffed the present, paper and all, into a shopping bag and set out across the river, toward town and the apartments across from campus.

It took twenty minutes to find the right apartment, and when she rang the bell, no one answered. It was still early.

She couldn't just leave the box out there in the hallway. The secretary wouldn't even know who it was from. Somebody might walk off with it. Finally, when Caroline was about to leave, she heard the chain slide off on the other side, and the door opened just a crack.

A sleepy-looking woman in a bathrobe stared down at Caroline.

"Are you Dad's secretary?" Caroline asked, and she realized she was on the verge of tears.

In turn, the secretary asked, "Are you one of the Malloy girls?"

"Yes," said Caroline. "I . . . I brought the present Dad was going to give *you* for Christmas. Mom picked it out. I think there's been a horrible mistake."

The secretary opened the door and invited her in. "Yes," she said, "I guess so."

There in the trash basket, just inside the door, was more angel wrapping paper and the box in which Caroline had placed the cat vomit.

"Do you want to sit down?" the woman asked, rubbing her eyes with two fingers.

Caroline sat, and her chin trembled.

"I'm really sorry," she said haltingly. "I was playing a trick on a boy at school, and somehow he got your present and you got his, and Dad doesn't know."

The secretary reached for the present in the shopping bag that was already unwrapped. Caroline had removed the note from Wally. There was only a note on the wrapping paper that said, "For all your precious memories. C. Malloy." The *C*, Caroline realized, stood for *Coach,* but how could Wally have known that?

"It's lovely," the secretary said. "I'll put my fiancé's letters in this. I *wondered* what I had ever done that would make your father send me such an awful thing for Christmas. In fact, I was about to call and ask him."

Caroline cringed.

"Tell me," the secretary went on, "who could you possibly dislike so much that you would send him cat puke with hairballs in it? *Mouse* feet, even?"

"Wally Hatford," Caroline answered.

"What did he ever do to deserve this?"

Caroline thought about it. She could remember a lot of things Wally had done to deserve it, but the strange thing was, everything she thought of had been kind of fun.

"I don't know," she said at last. "He's just fun to tease, that's all."

"Did he give *you* something awful for Christmas?"

"No. He didn't give me anything."

The woman smiled a little. "Well, I'm not sure *I* would have given you anything either. But I do appreciate your coming over with this, Caroline. Thank you. And I promise not to mention it to your dad."

Caroline walked thoughtfully back home, realizing how close she had come to disaster. If Wally had not returned the box—if he had not said anything at all—and if the secretary had called Caroline's father, things would have been in an even grander mess than they were already. She shivered in spite of her coat and mittens.

*I will never tease Wally Hatford again,* she vowed silently. *I will stop hating the Hatfords.* Actually, she'd never really hated them in the first place. They'd disgusted her and teased her, but she didn't hate them. In fact, when and if her dad decided to go back to Ohio with the family, she realized she would miss all the fun she'd had with them very much.

When she walked into the house, however, and smelled the comforting fragrance of the cookies Beth was baking, there sat Peter Hatford, a chocolate chip cookie in one hand, a lemon square in the other.

"Guess what, Caroline?" he said happily. "I've got two jobs!"

"Really?" said Caroline pleasantly, in her new role as friend to the Hatfords. "What are they?"

"I'm cookie taster for Beth. I have to taste one cookie from every batch she makes and see if she forgot the sugar or anything."

"Hey, how lucky can you get?" said Eddie darkly, raising her eyebrows at Caroline. "Tell Caroline what your other job is. Tell her who hired you."

"I'm a spy for Jake and Josh and Wally," said Peter. "I'm supposed to report everything you're doing here."

Caroline stared at Peter. "Then why did you tell us?"

"Because Beth said I could have all the cookies I could eat if I'd tell her why Jake sent me over here. She said it wouldn't make any difference, I could still tell them what you're doing."

"Great!" said Caroline, exchanging looks with Beth and Eddie and trying not to laugh. "And what will you tell them we're doing?"

"Making cookies," said Peter.

"And what else will you tell them?" prodded Beth. "Remember that little poem I taught you? What are little girls made of?"

" 'Sugar and spice, and all that's nice,' " said Peter.

"You got it!" said Eddie. "Tell your brothers that, and watch them go ballistic."

■ ■ ■ ■ ■ ■ ■ ■ ■ ■ ■ ■

# Twenty

■

# The Worst Christmas Ever

**W**ally knew it was going to be an awful Christmas. Three uncles and one aunt arrived on Christmas Eve and, as always, they brought an armload of presents. That was the nice part.

Mother roasted the big turkey for Christmas Eve dinner, one of the ones all the workers had received from their boss at the hardware store, and that was nice too. Especially the mince pies and chocolate cake.

It was even nice when Tom Hatford and his three brothers stood around the old upright piano after dinner, and while Aunt Vivian played, formed a quartet and sang carols. With his stomach full of turkey and rolls and mashed potatoes and chocolate cake, with a heap of presents waiting to be opened beneath the tree, how could anyone not feel cheerful? Wally asked himself.

*Easy*, he answered as the carols seemed to go on and

on. Wally, who did not sing, began to grow tired. He could not even go to bed because he and his brothers were sleeping on the living room floor that night in their sleeping bags, so until the uncles stopped singing, there was no sleep for anyone, not even Peter.

> *"God rest ye merry, gentlemen,*
> *Let nothing you dismay, . . ."*

The uncles sang, but as Wally's eyes began to close, as Christmas seemed to drift farther and farther away and Miss Applebaum seemed to float closer and closer, the words seemed to change:

> *God rest ye, little Hatford boy,*
> *For much to your dismay,*
> *Remember what Miss Applebaum*
> *Will open Christmas Day. . . .*

He put his hands over his ears to drown out the singing and was glad, when he crawled into his sleeping bag at last around eleven, that he felt himself finally drifting off into sleep.

Miss Applebaum was the biggest thing on his mind Christmas morning, however. He got the Pittsburgh Steelers sweatshirt that he wanted, and the Nikes, the computer game, and the book about vampire bats, but he knew that as soon as Christmas vacation was over, he would still have to go back to school and face both Caroline and his teacher.

He wasn't sure which would be worse. He had expected that Caroline would have put something really, really gross in the box she gave him, and it turned out to be a box for letters. *Love* letters, probably. Caroline Malloy was actually in *love* with him? Now he *knew* she was crazy.

Wally had given the box back, of course, but what if she wrote love letters to him anyway? Was he supposed to keep them? What if the other guys found out? He wasn't *ready* for love! He wasn't *ready* for a girlfriend—least of all Caroline.

"Dad," he said later after all the company had gone and he and his father were picking up the wrapping paper. "Have you ever thought about living somewhere else?"

"Where did you have in mind, Wally?" asked his father. "You want me to move down the block, maybe?"

"No, I mean all of us. I mean . . . well, the Bensons moved to Georgia and the Malloys moved here, and I just wondered if *we* might ever go live somewhere else."

"Can't see any reason to," his father replied. "I have a perfectly good job with the post office, your mother works in the hardware store, Buckman seems like a fine place to raise boys, and we have a lot of friends here. No, we don't have any plans to move."

It was when Wally thought of facing his teacher, however, that he thought of running away.

Not only had he never given a girl a Christmas present, he was not a boy who gave teachers presents either. It was not just the thought of what Miss Applebaum would think when she opened the present

Mom had delivered and found Wally's underpants, it was what she would *do*.

What if he walked into Miss Applebaum's class the first day after Christmas vacation and she had all her gifts lined up on her desk—a new coffee mug, a paperweight, a pencil holder, a vase . . . And what if she thanked each person out loud and showed the gift to the class? What if, at the very end, she said, "And then, from Wally Hatford, I received this very strange present . . ." and held up his underpants for all the class to see? Underpants with a happy face drawn on the seat?

Wally didn't think he could stand it.

He even tried calling his teacher to explain, but there was no Applebaum listed in the phone book. Maybe she didn't live in Buckman. Or maybe she was unlisted so that boys who went around giving their teachers underpants couldn't bother them over school vacations.

In the days that followed Christmas, Wally—who was usually happiest by himself, just lying on his back studying a spiderweb, or dragging a stick in the river—found he was happiest *not* being alone, because when he was alone, he started to think, and when he thought, there was only one thing that came to mind. Two, actually: Caroline and Miss Applebaum.

On one of the days, when Jake and Josh were busy doing other things and even Peter was busy playing with the toys he got for Christmas, Wally walked downtown, where shoppers were busy returning presents they didn't want or looking for after-Christmas bargains.

He strolled through the five-and-dime, wandered through the drugstore, and was looking through the paperbacks on a rack in Oldakers' Bookstore when he looked up to see Caroline Malloy standing on the other side of the rack, looking straight at him.

Caroline spun the rack to the left and picked up a paperback. Wally spun the rack to the right. He didn't walk away just then or she'd know she'd scared him away, and Wally couldn't bear for her to think that.

*Why* did she move here anyway? Why did she have to be in his class? Why did she have to be precocious?

Wally realized, however, that she was going to be here eight more months at least—eight months, perhaps, before he knew if the Bensons were coming back or not. And if he didn't make peace with her soon, no telling what might happen.

Both he and Caroline opened their mouths at the same time.

"I shouldn't . . . ," said Wally.

"I didn't . . . ," said Caroline.

They each stopped.

"What?" said Wally. He saw Caroline swallow.

"I didn't mean to give you that box," said Caroline. "It was supposed to go to Dad's secretary."

"He's giving his secretary a box for love letters?" asked Wally.

"Not *his* love letters. She's engaged to be married, and Mom picked the present out, and I got the boxes mixed up."

Wally thought that over. Well, *that* was a relief. "What *did* you mean to give me?"

"Uh . . . well, that was a mistake too. The secretary got it."

"What was it?"

"You don't want to know."

Was Caroline laughing? Wally wondered. He found that he was starting to smile himself. "Yes I do," he said.

"Cat puke," said Caroline. "With a big fat hairball in it and undigested mouse feet."

Wally's eyes opened wide. "That went to your dad's secretary?"

"Yep."

Wally laughed out loud. Then he thought of Miss Applebaum opening the present intended for Caroline, and he stopped.

"Miss Applebaum got yours, and I'm in big trouble," he said.

Now Caroline looked curious. "What was it?" she asked.

"Those underpants you wore to give your report." He grinned again. "With the happy face on the seat of the pants. And a note saying, 'Since you liked them so much, you can have them.' "

And suddenly Wally and Caroline were both laughing. *Together.*

"Do you think she's opened it yet?" asked Caroline.

"Of course. It's after Christmas."

"What are you going to do?"

Wally shrugged. "Catch the first Greyhound out of town. Oh, man, that first day back at school I'm gonna be dead meat."

Caroline moved around the paperback rack until she was beside Wally. Looking right into his eyes, in fact.

"Why don't I go get them back?" she asked.

"What?"

"When vacation's over, I'll go up to her desk and just ask for them back."

"You will?"

"Sure. I'll tell her they were meant for me."

"Okay," said Wally. "Thanks."

As he walked home later, Wally could not quite believe what had just happened. He didn't tell anyone at home about it, Jake in particular. Peter, of course, liked the girls. Josh—he wasn't sure. But Jake? No way. Nevertheless, he began to think that maybe it had been a pretty good Christmas after all.

■

When Monday came, Wally walked into his classroom and hung up his jacket. He sat down at his desk and got out his math book and pencil. But when he looked up, there was Miss Applebaum looking at him, her gray eyes staring right through him. Wally felt his backbone folding like an accordion. He seemed to be sinking lower and lower in his seat.

And then, before he could say a word—explain or apologize—he heard Caroline rise from her seat behind him and saw her walk to the front of the room. While the other kids were still hanging up their jackets and milling around, Caroline faced the teacher and said, "Miss Applebaum, I think you got a present meant for me. It was from Wally Hatford. I wondered if I could have it."

She did it. Caroline actually did it! She *liked* doing things like this. Liked going up to the front of the room and doing something a little bit brave or dramatic or wild.

"Oh?" said Miss Applebaum. "And what would that be, I wonder?"

"Well, actually, it was a pair of underpants," Caroline said.

"Yes?" said Miss Applebaum.

"With a happy face drawn on the seat."

Was Miss Applebaum smiling? Wally wondered. She was certainly trying not to.

"And a note that said, 'Since you liked them so much, you can have them,' " added Caroline.

Wally swallowed.

"And he really meant this weird little present for you?" asked Miss Applebaum, looking surprised.

"I guess so. It was just a joke," said Caroline in a voice as soft and meek and polite as a kitten. *She can really act!* Wally thought, impressed.

Miss Applebaum reached down and opened the lower drawer of her desk. "Very well," she said, taking out the square box, minus the angel wrapping paper, and handing it to Caroline. "Since you seem to know the contents so well, it's obviously yours. You may have it."

"Thank you," said Caroline.

She walked back toward Wally, deposited the box on his desk, smiled sweetly, and said, "For you, since you obviously like them so much." And then she laughed, and Wally smiled, and he began to wonder: Who was the Crazie? Caroline or him?

■ ■ ■ ■ ■ ■ ■ ■ ■ ■

# Twenty-one

■

# Paying the Debt

Caroline did not tell her sisters what she had done for Wally. She didn't even tell them what Wally had been planning to give her. It was a secret—a secret between Wally and Caroline.

For the rest of the week, she did not want to poke Wally in the back, bump his shoulder, tweak his ear, or run her ruler along the back of his neck. The Hatfords and the Malloys pretty much stayed to themselves. Until Sunday morning, that is, when Buckman awoke to four inches of snow.

The girls were awakened by their father, who poked his head into every bedroom in turn.

"Eddie?" he called. Then, "Beth? Caroline?"

And when each girl rose up on her elbow and looked at him, he said, "It snowed again, it's Sunday morning, and there are three snow shovels in the garage. It's a good way to earn some money to pay off your debt, so I suggest you get up now."

There were groans and whispered protests from the three bedrooms, but the girls had no choice except to pull themselves out of bed, into their sweatpants and sweatshirts, and, after a hot oatmeal breakfast, to stagger sleepily out to the garage. They stood looking at the three snow shovels lined up like sentries against one wall.

"I don't even know how much to charge," Eddie said, her shoulders hunched, hands in her pockets. "We never had to do this before."

"Five dollars a house?" Caroline suggested.

"Even if we did every house on Island Avenue, we wouldn't have enough to pay the rest of what we owe," said Beth.

All three girls were grumpy at being awakened, and Eddie, in particular, had that look in her eye.

"Let's go across the river and knock on the Hatfords' door," she said.

Beth looked at her incredulously. *"Why?"*

"Just to make them feel guilty," she said. "To show them that we're up and working while they're still lazing around. That we can shovel just as fast as they can."

"Yeah, let's!" said Beth.

With shovels over their shoulders like workers in a salt mine, the girls traipsed down the hill and across the river on the swinging bridge, icicles hanging off the cable handrails like teeth.

There was no sign of activity at the Hatfords' or any other house on the street. The Hatfords' newspaper was still lying on a heap of snow out by the road.

Beth picked up the paper, and the girls waded through the snow and clomped up the steps onto the porch. Beth knocked.

They could hear a chair scrape the floor inside, then footsteps, and finally Mrs. Hatford opened the door, followed by Jake.

"Why, my goodness, it's the Malloy girls, at eight o'clock in the morning!" she said. "Won't you come in and have some cocoa?"

Jake backed up as though afraid that they might, and Caroline noticed that he was still wearing his pajama bottoms and T-shirt.

"No, thank you," said Beth. "We just wondered if you wanted your sidewalk and steps shoveled. Only five dollars."

"Well, aren't you the early birds, though!" Mrs. Hatford declared. "And here I have four boys with strong backs, who—"

"We're trying to earn money we sort of owe our dad," said Caroline in her most pitiable voice. "So we thought we'd start with you."

"Oh, well, in that case . . . Ordinarily I'd have the boys do the shoveling, but . . . You girls go right ahead, and when you're through, come inside for the five dollars and some cocoa as well."

*"Mom!"* Jake wailed, but the door closed, and Eddie, Beth, and Caroline exchanged grins as they thrust their shovels into the snow on the steps and began to scrape and push. They could hear pounding footsteps from inside and knew that Jake was waking up Josh and Wally and Peter, and together the four boys were probably looking out a window at them right now.

"I'll bet they just can't *stand* this!" Beth said. "*Us!* Doing the shoveling for *them!*"

"I don't know about that," said Caroline. "Maybe they can stand it very well. Maybe they *love* to see us work."

But Eddie agreed with Beth. "They'll be embarrassed as anything. Imagine having the neighbors see *girls* shoveling the sidewalk for *boys!*"

"What do you bet they come out and order us to go home?" said Beth.

"Well, if you're right, they'll probably come out and do it for us. They'll just have to prove they're stronger and bigger and smarter and faster, when they're really dumber than doorbells and slower than snails," said Eddie.

They had finished the steps and half the sidewalk when suddenly the front door opened and out came Jake and Josh, followed by Wally and Peter, all wearing boots and jackets and mittens and caps.

"Don't let them push us off," whispered Eddie. "No matter what they say, their mom said we can do it."

"Shovel faster!" murmured Caroline.

"Don't even look at them," said Beth.

Caroline was shoveling as fast as she could when four pairs of boots appeared in front of her, and she looked up to see the Hatford brothers looking back. Looking at her and Beth and Eddie.

"Need some help?" asked Josh.

"No," said Eddie.

"Really?" Josh said.

"We're doing just fine," Eddie responded.

"I know, but how are you going to do all the other houses on the street? Mom said you're trying to earn some money . . ."

"So what?" said Eddie. "We can do the sidewalks up one side of the street and down the other all by ourselves."

*"Eddie!"* whispered Beth. "We can't!"

"Well, we thought maybe you'd like us to help," Josh told her. "I mean, you could do one side of the street and we'll do the other. Or maybe we could work together on the same driveway."

"Yeah? And you guys walk off with all the money? No way!" said Eddie.

Wally spoke up next: "What if we said you could have all the money?"

Eddie, Beth, and Caroline stared at the four boys as though they had sprung four new heads.

"You've got to be kidding," said Caroline.

"No, we're not!" Peter piped up. "Josh said we're going to help you so you won't be mad at us anymore."

"Shut up, Peter," Josh muttered.

"Well, if you're going to help, then help. Don't just stand there gabbing," Eddie snapped, still not trusting. She dumped a shovelful of snow so close to Wally's feet she could have buried him had he been any closer.

In response, Wally dug up a shovelful of snow and dumped it close to where Eddie was standing. Then the four boys began madly shoveling snow, dumping it as close to the girls as they could get without actually touching them, and the girls madly shoveled back.

In less than two minutes, the rest of the Hatfords' sidewalk was as clean as a bald-headed baby.

"Well!" said Beth when she looked around and discovered that they were at the end of the sidewalk. "*That* didn't take long."

Josh walked down the road to the next house and knocked on the door.

"Shovel your steps and walk?" he asked. "Only five dollars to have it done in five minutes? Driveway's five bucks extra."

"Five minutes?" said the neighbor, looking out. "I *wondered* how I'd get to church this morning! Okay, it's a deal."

And so it went. People who had never paid before to have someone shovel their walk and driveway paid five or ten dollars just to have it done in five minutes.

It got to be a game after a while. Who could do their side of the walk or driveway faster, the boys or the girls? Who could dump their snow closest to the other side without actually dumping it on anyone? It wasn't long before they had earned forty dollars.

Only when Peter began to complain that his feet were cold did Caroline realize they hadn't collected yet from Mrs. Hatford. And so, some of them dragging their shovels, others with shovels over their shoulders, they headed back up the block, their breath frosty in front of them, and slogged through the snow to the Hatfords'.

"Hey!" said Peter, cheerful now that they were going back to get warm. "I have a great idea! We could have sort of a business! Whenever it snows, we could go out together and make a lot of money!"

"Yeah, and give it all to the girls," Jake said dryly.

"Why not?" said Eddie. "We're worth it."

"Ha!" said Wally. "You give these girls money, they buy you presents like boxes filled with cat puke and mouse feet." He grinned at Caroline.

"You should talk!" said Caroline. "You were going to give me a pair of underpants. *Your* underpants."

"But *you* were trying to trap us in the garage," said Wally.

"We wouldn't have done it if you hadn't been spying on us from the loft in the first place," said Eddie.

"We wouldn't have been meeting up there if we didn't think you were plotting something new just to bug us," said Josh.

A car was pulling up into the Hatfords' driveway just as the three Malloy girls and the four Hatfords came dragging their shovels along the sidewalk.

They stopped and watched the car.

The driver's door opened. One booted foot came out and settled itself on the driveway, then the other foot, a hand, a head, until finally a woman in a blue coat was out of the car and looking around.

"Well, hi, Wally! Jake! Josh! And Peter, too. My goodness, how *are* you?" the woman said. "Would you believe I haven't worn boots since we moved to Georgia?"

The boys were speechless and could only stand and stare, because there, going up their sidewalk to the front porch, was Mrs. Benson, mother of their five best friends, the best friends the Hatfords had in the whole wide world. Well, maybe.

■ ■ ■ ■ ■ ■ ■ ■ ■ ■ ■

# Twenty-two

■

# Company

When Mrs. Benson saw the girls, however, she stopped and looked them over.

"Would these be Coach Malloy's daughters, by chance?" she asked Wally.

"Yes," he said.

Mrs. Benson studied them over the rim of her glasses. "I see!" she said, and went on up the steps. Mrs. Hatford was holding open the door.

"She *knows*!" breathed Wally.

"Knows what?" asked Eddie suspiciously.

But Wally only swallowed.

"Did you write the Bensons and tell on the girls?" whispered Josh accusingly.

Jake, however, looked hopeful. "Maybe they're coming back!" he said. He ran up the steps after Mrs. Benson, and Wally and Josh followed wordlessly, leaving the girls staring after them on the sidewalk.

Mother was hugging Mrs. Benson in the hallway, and Dad was saying, "Well, Shirley, this is a surprise!"

"Actually, I'm spending the weekend with my sister in Elkins," Mrs. Benson explained, "but I thought it might be a good idea to check on things here, especially after the letters the boys got from Wally."

Wally swallowed again.

"Letters?" said Mother. "What letters?"

"The letter about how Caroline tried to kill Beth, I'll bet!" said Peter helpfully.

"You know," said Dad, "I think we should sit down at the kitchen table and have a cup of coffee." And when he saw Wally edging toward the stairs, he said, "You guys are included. Have some orange juice."

The grown-ups sat at one end of the big country table in the kitchen, the four boys at the other, while Mrs. Benson drank her coffee.

"We just didn't know what to make of it, those girls throwing hammers around up in the bedroom and painting our garage. Granted, it's old, but it served us well, and I'd think that a man employed by the college—a coach, in particular—would let us know if he wanted to make changes on our property."

Father looked at Wally.

"I guess I exaggerate a little," Wally said.

"I guess you do," said his father. "Suppose you start at the beginning."

Jake was giving Wally his "traitor" look, but Josh seemed to be nodding, urging him on, so Wally explained: "We were holding club meetings up in the

143

loft just to bug the girls, and they decided to trap us up there. So Eddie got some paint and painted the ladder, and when we started to come down we got paint on our clothes."

"What?" said Mother.

"Don't worry. We got it out with turpentine," Wally said. "Then, when Mr. Malloy came home, he got some on his sport jacket and now the girls have to earn money to pay for it, that's all. All they painted were the rungs of the ladder. And they've really taken pretty good care of the place."

"My goodness, you *do* exaggerate, don't you!" Mrs. Benson said.

Wally hoped that once the truth was out, that might be the end of it. He thought now that he'd told how it really happened, Mrs. Benson would say, *Well, then, I see there's nothing to worry about!* and go back to Georgia.

She sipped her coffee thoughtfully for a moment, then said, "It's hard being away from your own house for so long. I wanted to feel at home in Georgia, and in some ways I do—the boys seem to like it a lot— but I miss Buckman. I suppose if we come back, I'll miss Georgia too."

"Has Hal made a decision yet?" Father asked.

"Not really. He's had one offer from the college where he's teaching now, and he's waiting to hear from some other schools before he decides. I suppose it could go either way. It would just be nice to know that if we *do* come back to Buckman, though, there will be a house to come home *to.*"

Jake and Josh, Wally, and Peter, excused themselves

as soon as they thought they could get away, and made a beeline for the stairs. Once they got to Jake and Josh's bedroom, they closed the door and sat down on the beds.

"Wally, you jerk!" Josh said, still mad that he'd told on the girls.

But Jake asked, "What are we going to do if the Bensons don't come back?"

"What are we going to do if they *do*?" said Josh.

"What do you mean?" asked Jake.

"Come on, Jake, the girls have been fun and you know it," said Josh.

"Yeah, but we used to play ball with the guys every evening in the summer!"

"We can play ball with the girls," said Josh. "Eddie especially."

"We used to explore the cove and fool around the old coal mine," Jake protested.

"We can explore them with the Malloys," said Wally.

"The girls are nice!" piped up Peter. "They make good cookies!"

Jake threw back his head in exasperation. "What's happened to you guys? You've been brainwashed! You *know* we've been waiting for the Bensons to come back! We *always* wanted the Bensons to come back."

"Maybe we can have both," said Wally. "Maybe the Bensons will come back and the Malloys will stay."

"Not likely," said Jake. "Buckman isn't that big a place. They don't need two football coaches at the college."

The boys sat morosely on the beds, staring at each other.

"The thing is," said Josh, "Coach Malloy might ask his family what they want him to do. If they all hate it here, they'll probably go back. If the girls really want to stay, though, maybe he will."

"You think they'll want to stay after all we've done to them?" asked Wally.

"Hey! They'll probably stay *because* of what we've done. They had as much fun as we did," Josh told him.

Wally walked out in the hall to see whether Mrs. Benson had left yet, to go check on her house. She was still downstairs. In fact, she was on the phone in the hallway at that very moment, talking to Mrs. Malloy.

"Well, I'm glad to know you're enjoying our house," he heard her say. "I didn't want to just come barging over with no warning at all, but I did want to see it. I wondered if there was anything needing repair. . . . I see. . . . Yes. . . . Well, that's fine then. . . . Of course. I'll come by."

Upstairs, the boys crowded around the door, listening.

When Mrs. Benson hung up, she said, "Well, I'm going over there and see for myself if they're taking care of things. Once you open your house to renters, you have no idea what's happening to it, do you?"

"I'm afraid not," said Mother. "But I feel quite sure the Malloys are responsible people, Shirley."

"I hope so," said Mrs. Benson.

The boys watched from the crack in the door as

Mrs. Benson pulled on her coat again, went out the door, and drove her sister's car around to the road bridge, and the Malloys' on Island Avenue. For the next hour and a half, they didn't leave the bedroom. Using their father's binoculars, they watched out an upstairs window, half expecting to see a moving van pull up Island Avenue and all the Malloys pile out of the house with their furniture, to go back to Ohio.

Instead, they finally saw Mrs. Benson come out of the house. She went into the garage for a minute, then came back out and got into the car.

"What do you suppose happened?" breathed Wally.

"I don't know," said Jake.

"We could call and find out," Josh suggested.

Jake shook his head.

And then all eyes fell upon Peter.

"They never did get their five dollars for shoveling our sidewalk," said Josh. "Peter, how about you taking it over to them along with a note?"

"Sure!" said Peter. "Every time I go to their house I get cookies!"

So Wally went downstairs and got the five dollars from his mother, along with a lecture.

"What goes on in the Malloy house is strictly between them and the Bensons, and you shouldn't be telling tales," Mother said. "If you can't write a letter without exaggerating, Wally, don't write one at all."

Wally went back upstairs with the money, and Josh wrapped it up in a piece of notebook paper on which he had written, *So, are you guys getting kicked out or what?*

"Give it to one of the girls, Peter, not the parents. Okay?" Jake instructed.

Peter stuffed the note with the five dollars in his pocket, and his brothers watched as he went across the front lawn in his boots and parka toward the swinging bridge.

In summer, when leaves were on the trees, you could hardly see the Malloy house unless you went through the trapdoor in the attic and up onto the widow's walk on the roof. But now, with the trees bare, they could see many things across the river they couldn't see at any other time. Still, the binoculars helped.

They watched as Peter shuffled along. Every few feet he scraped the snow away with one boot to see what was beneath it. All along the swinging bridge, he ran his hand along the cable handrail to push off the snow. Every so often he stopped to throw a handful of snow into the river, then leaned over to see where it landed on the ice.

"If he went any slower, he'd be crawling," said Jake.

"If he went any slower, it would be Monday by the time he got there," said Josh.

"If he went any slower, the Malloys could be moved out and back to Ohio," Wally observed.

It had begun to snow again, and big frosty flakes drifted down from the sky. The boys groaned as Peter stopped in the middle of the bridge again, his head thrown back, and tried to collect snowflakes on his tongue.

Finally he reached the other side and slowly made

his way up the hill to the Malloy house, taking two steps up the steep slope of their back lawn, sliding one step back, taking two steps more, sliding one step back, before he disappeared in the snow and fog.

An hour went by. An hour and fifteen minutes. An hour and a half.

"What could he be *doing* over there?" groaned Josh. "What'd he do, take a suitcase? Is he moving in?"

The snow continued to fall. There was now almost an inch and a half on the window ledge.

"I want you boys to shovel that sidewalk before it gets any deeper," Mother called up the stairs.

"What? We already did it once! You paid the girls to do it!" Jake protested.

"Well, it's got to be done again," Mother said.

Just then they saw Peter coming back across the bridge. It took him about as long to get home again as it had taken him to cross in the first place.

Finally, when he opened the front door and began stomping his feet in the hallway, Jake and Josh rushed down and brought him up so fast he didn't even have time to get his boots off. There was chocolate syrup around his mouth. Cookie crumbs on his jacket. Peter looked dazed and happy and kind of sleepy.

"What did they *say*?" asked Josh.

"Are they leaving?" asked Jake.

"Did Mrs. Benson tell them they had to move?" Wally wanted to know.

In answer, Peter pulled a note out of his pocket and handed it to Wally. Wally read it silently first, then swallowed, and read it aloud to his brothers:

*So you were the ones who told the Bensons about the "murder" up in Beth's room, and our "painting the garage"! And now you want to know whether we're leaving or not. You want to know whether we're going back to Ohio and if your old buddies will be back from Georgia.*

*Well, you know what? We're not going to tell you. And if you think it was hard waiting for Peter to get back across the bridge with this note, just think what it will be like waiting till next summer for your answer!*

*Eddie, Beth, and Caroline*

*P.S. Thanks for your help in shoveling the sidewalks.*

*Double P.S. Did you notice it's snowing again?*
*Did you notice we took your shovels?*
*Did you know it will cost you five dollars to get them back?*

*The Whomper, the Weirdo, and the Crazie*

## Read all about the Hatford boys and the Malloy girls.

### The Boys Start the War

Just when the Hatford brothers are expecting three boys to move into the house across the river where their best friends used to live, the Malloy girls arrive instead. Wally and his brothers decide to make Caroline and her sisters so miserable that they'll want to go back to Ohio, but they haven't counted on the ingenuity of the girls. From dead fish to dead bodies, floating cakes to floating heads, the pranks continue—first by the boys, then by the girls—until someone is taken prisoner!

### The Girls Get Even

Still smarting from the boys' latest trick, the girls are determined to get even. Caroline is thrilled to play the part of Goblin Queen in the school play, especially since Wally Hatford has to be her footman. The boys, however, have a creepy plan for Halloween night. They're certain the girls will walk right into their trap. Little do the boys know what the Malloy sisters have in store.

### Boys Against Girls

Abaguchie mania! Caroline Malloy shivers happily when her on-again, off-again enemy Wally Hatford tells her that the remains of a strange animal known as the abaguchie have been spotted in their area. Wally swears Caroline to secrecy and warns her not to search by herself. But Caroline will do anything to find the secret of the bones and finds out the hard way that she should have listened.

### The Girls' Revenge

Christmas is coming, but Caroline Malloy and Wally Hatford aren't singing carols around the tree. Instead, these sworn enemies must interview each other for the dreaded December class project. Caroline, as usual, has a trick up her sleeve that's sure to shock Wally. In the meantime, Wally and his brothers find a way to spy on the Malloy girls at home. The girls vow to get revenge on those sneaky Hatfords with a trap the boys won't soon forget.

## A Traitor Among the Boys

The Hatford boys make a New Year's resolution to treat the Malloy girls like sisters. But who says you can't play tricks on sisters? The girls will need to stay one step ahead of the boys and are willing to pay big-time for advance information. Homemade cookies should be all it takes to make a traitor spill the beans. In the meantime, Caroline is delighted with her role in the town play. Don't ask how Beth, Josh, and Wally get roped into it—just wait until showtime, when Caroline pulls her wildest stunt yet!

## A Spy Among the Girls

Valentine's Day is coming up, and love is in the air for Beth Malloy and Josh Hatford. When they're spotted holding hands, Josh tells his teasing brothers that he's simply spying on the girls to see what they're plotting next. At the same time, Caroline Malloy, the family actress, decides she must know what it's like to fall in love. Poor Wally Hatford is in for it when she chooses him as the object of her affection!

## The Boys Return

It's spring break, and the only assignment Wally Hatford and Caroline Malloy have is to do something they've never done before. Wally's sure that will be a cinch, because the mighty Benson brothers are coming. It will be nonstop action all the way. For starters, the nine Benson and Hatford boys plan to scare the three Malloy sisters silly by convincing them that their house is haunted. Meanwhile, everyone in town has heard that there's a hungry cougar on the prowl. When the kids decide to take a break from their tricks and join forces to catch the cougar, guess who gets stuck with the scariest job?

## The Girls Take Over

The Hatford boys and the Malloy girls are ready to outdo each other again. Eddie is the first girl ever to try out for the school baseball team. Now she and Jake are vying for the same position, while Caroline and Wally compete to become class spelling champ. As if that's not enough, the kids decide to race bottles down the rising Buckman River to see whose will travel farthest by the end of the month. Of course, neither team trusts the other, and when the girls go down to the river to capture the boys' bottles, well . . . it looks as if those Malloy girls may be in over their heads this time!

## Boys in Control

Wally Hatford always seems to get a raw deal. The rest of the family goes to the ball game, and he has to stay home to watch over a yard sale. Caroline Malloy writes a silly play for a school project, and he gets roped into costarring in it with her! Things are looking down, especially when the Malloy girls stumble across an embarrassing item from the boys' past. But Wally finally gets his chance to turn the tables on the girls' scheme and prove who's really in control. Boys rule!

## Girls Rule!

The rivalry between the Malloy sisters and the Hatford boys is heating up! The kids have two weeks to earn money for a fundraising contest. All those who collect twenty dollars or more for the new children's wing at the hospital can be in the annual Strawberry Festival Parade or get lots of strawberry treats. The only place Caroline wants to be is on the Strawberry Queen's float. How will she earn the money in time? Do the Hatfords have moneymaking secrets they're not telling the girls?

## Boys Rock!

Wally, the best speller among the Hatford brothers, gets roped into helping them with a summer newspaper project that will earn the twins school credit. Mr. Oldaker trusts Wally to keep a secret that could turn into a scoop for their newspaper, but Wally worries that the secret may be too scary to keep to himself. What's worse, the Malloy girls have horned in on the newspaper. If there's one person Wally won't spill his secret to, it's nutty Caroline Malloy. No matter what it is!